In loving memory of Dr Shoab Ibrahim and
Dr Saad Al-Dujaily, two brothers in heaven.

Dear TK,

Keep striving young king!
Your dedication will shine through.

— Ranis

Prelude

29th *December 2014*

A light fog descended over the Merton and Surrey cemetery. It was the funeral of Harry Moffat, a loving father and husband who had suddenly passed away from a vicious heart attack. He had lived with his family in the heart of Chelsea. A respected and successful doctor, he would go above and beyond for his patients. He had saved the lives of hundreds but had impacted the lives of thousands more. He was also one of the most generous and thoughtful men to ever walk this earth. He had been taken too early, but, as they say, angels aren't meant to walk in this world; they belong in heaven, which is undoubtedly where his soul had now gone to rest. Hundreds were in attendance to say goodbye to an inspirational doctor. The coffin in which he lay had an ironic gleam to it, despite the murky conditions. As people mourned, the coffin was about to be lowered.

Among the crowd of people gathered were two 12-year-old boys standing one on either side of the coffin, challenged with the task of burying their dad. As they were instructed on how to lift the coffin, the two locked eyes. They had never met each other yet were so similar they almost seemed to understand each other. The two examined every inch of their opposite number as if they were supposed to have come into contact yet never had. The standout feature of the two was their eyes, yet there was a slight difference. One's eyes were full of hope and opportunity, but the other's were filled with defeat and despair.

The coffin was raised then slowly lowered to its final resting place. As the coffin struck the ground, reality hit all in attendance. He was really gone. The two boys locked eyes again as they were asked to throw the first soil onto the coffin, a tradition that demanded maturity beyond their years. They each threw their handful of soil and took a step back from the ever-descending hole. The two boys continue to stare at each other but were soon whisked away by their respective mothers. They both turned to take one last look at the other. This is the story of two brothers.

Part 1

Ross Susans sat on the end of his rickety old bed. The 17-year-old was blasting Catfish and the Bottlemen's latest song while desperately trying to cram the last bit of revision in before his first A-Level mock exam. He stared emptily at the Philosophy textbook in front of him, trying to understand the cycle of samsara. He was halfway down the page when he heard a knock on his bedroom door.

"*Ross!*" his mum yelled. "*You're going to be late!*"

Ross glanced down at his watch, surprised to see that it had hit 8:45. He leapt off his bed, throwing his crusty headphones into his bag and launching his textbook across the room. He lasered out the door and burst into the kitchen. Ross lived with his mum and his older brother, Reece, in a small council estate just outside Harold Wood. The whole flat took no more space than one living room in a normal house. The kitchen was only slyly bigger than his bedroom. He went to kiss his mum goodbye and slapped his brother before leaving the flat.

He was met with the frosty wind of a normal October day but also a croaky voice.

"*Yo, Sus!*"

He recognised the voice almost instantly. It was Harry "Crackhead" Smith. Since Ross could remember, Harry had been his neighbour. He had been given the name Crackhead around the estate as everyone was aware that he made crystal meth in his

1

flat and used the youngers on the estate as his runners. The crazy thing about Harry was that he tested his supply on himself, which made him both unpredictable and prone to violence. Ross always tried to avoid him as much as possible.

"*Where you off to so early, boy?*" Harry enquired.

"*Somewhere you should have stayed at,*" Ross snapped back.

"*What did you say to me?*"

"*You heard.*"

Ross turned to walk away but heard footsteps accelerating behind him. He turned sharply to see the crackhead staring him down only two inches away from his face.

"*You better watch how you speak to me, boy. I might have to cut off your brother's supply.*"

"*My brother doesn't touch your shit. Shut up.*"

"*You might want to check his room.*"

The crackhead took a few steps backwards before walking away with a heinous laugh that echoed around the estate. Ross stood perplexed for a minute before realising he was now even later. He assumed Harry was just trying to play with his mind again and dashed off down the stairs and towards his school.

Luke Moffat stared at his 50-inch TV, watching the latest instalment of his favourite show, Suits. In his hand, he had a freshly rolled zoot and began to search for his lighter. He opened the drawer of his expensive mahogany cabinet and was surprised to find all of his lighters were missing. In a fit of rage, he marched down the stairs in search of his mother.

"*Isobel!*" he yelled. "*Where the fuck are my lighters?*"

"*I've told you not to talk to me like that, Luke. You call me Mum.*"

"*Shut the fuck up. Where are they?*"

"*I threw them out. Come on, Luke, it's 9 am.*"

"*You fucking bitch. Now I have to go and get another one. Give me your card.*"

"*No, Luke.*"

"*I'll just take it then.*"

Luke reached for her bag at the same time as she did. He used his superior strength to wrestle it from her and took the card out of her wallet before storming out of the house, leaving her on the floor.

"*Stupid bitch,*" he muttered.

Luke walked out of his grand door and proceeded down the street. His all-black Nike tracksuit stood in stark contrast to the sensational houses he was walking past. He lived in one of the most affluent areas of Chelsea with his mum and sister, Georgia.

As Luke returned from the shop with five new lighters, he lit the zoot.

"*What the fuck do you want, Georgia?*"

"*We talked about how you talk to Mum. It's not right.*"

"*Yeah, well she shouldn't have thrown my shit away.*"

"*It wasn't yours! She bought them.*"

"*If you're gonna lecture me, Geo, I'm gonna leave.*"

"*Are you going to school today?*"

"*School is a place for idiots.*"

"*So, you're just going to stay here and get high... Think about what Dad would –*"

"*Finish that sentence and I'll throw you through that glass pane.*"

"*But –*"

"*But nothing – he's dead. He left us. End of.*"

Luke brushed Georgia aside before marching back up to his room and slamming the door behind him.

Ross sprinted toward Harold Wood Grammar and burst through the doors at 9:05, five minutes after his mock had started. As he entered the classroom, every pair of eyes turned to him.

"*Mr Susans! Late again,*" Dr Peters exclaimed.

"*I'm sorry, sir, I was caught up outside –*"

"*No excuses, Mr Susans. I'm deducting five marks.*"

"*But sir, I was –*"

"*Save it. I don't appreciate tardiness and laziness. Both of which traits you seem to have in abundance.*"

"*Sorry, Sir,*" Ross said sarcastically as he walked over to his seat.

"*And sort out your uniform! Just because you are poor doesn't mean you have to look it!*"

He chuckled and even managed to draw a few laughs from the rest of the class. Ross was ready to explode but he kept his emotions at bay to avoid any further punishment. He sat down and opened the paper.

In a flash, the time was up. Ross had finished the paper a whole half hour early and sat looking smug the rest of the time. Although most of the teachers looked down on him, Ross was one of the most hardworking students in the school, with an exceptional range of knowledge and a rare ability to convey it, which made him stand out from the rest of the students. He always felt that the teachers and his peers were simply jealous of him because he was more intelligent than they were. Before he left the classroom, he had a quiet chat with Dr Peters.

"*I didn't appreciate that comment, sir.*"

"*Well maybe if your dad had worked harder, I wouldn't have had to make it.*"

"*You know nothing about him. It was my mum who raised me, actually, and I know for a fact that she works harder than you do every day.*"

"*I seriously doubt that.*"

"I'll report you."

"And who will they believe? An Oxford-educated professor? Or you – a lazy boy who is arrogant beyond belief and isn't going anywhere?"

Ross pushed away from his desk and stormed out of the classroom. He kept his head down as he went to his next lesson. He always tried to keep himself to himself as he felt that no one could understand him or even converse at the same level. This made him appear anti-social and self-centred, which also made him a prime target.

Ross's next lesson was History. He had always had a flair for the creative subjects, the subjects where he could express his opinion and there was no definitive right or wrong answer. His mind liked working like that; he hated closed-ended questions. As he walked in, he was surprised to see the class had been set out differently. He had forgotten that today was mock trial day and he was second chair in the case. His class were recreating the case of the Unabomber – Ted Kaczynski. Ross rushed over to his seat next to his classmate, Jamal Bunghez. Jamal was one of the most popular students at the school, a top athlete and very active on the social scene. Ross never really got along with Jamal; he didn't trust him but was forced to work with him, having been put with him for this case.

"Have you got the stuff, Ross?" Jamal enquired.

"Yeah, of course."

Ross searched through his bag but realised that in his rush that morning he must have left his notes at home.

"Shit," Ross muttered.

"What?"

"I've left them at home."

"Fuck sake, Ross, you really are useless."

"It's fine, I remember it all."

"Bro, that's 15 pages of our defence."

"I've got it, don't worry."

The trial began, and the opposition started strong. Chloe Mitchener was the prosecutor – a straight A* student and teacher's pet. She went on the offensive instantly and seemed to tear apart any defence that Ross and Jamal would have had. She went with the narrative that the Unabomber was a stone-cold killer with no other objective than to harm others. Jamal tried his best to counter these points, but without Ross's notes, his arguments were incoherent and the jury didn't seem to be swayed. The judge then called a 10-minute recess before closing statements.

"Let me make the closing argument," suggested Ross.

"Are you out of your mind? You're second chair. You'll fuck this up for us. You've already done enough – she's basically won."

"Trust me."

"No, I'm doing it, Ross."

Ross rushed off to his seat.

"Is defence ready for closing statements?" the judge inquired.

"Yes, your honour," Ross replied with confidence.

"What the fuck are you doing, Ro –"

Before Jamal could finish his sentence, Ross leapt out of his seat and went to approach the jury.

"The opposition will have you believe this man is a cold-hearted murderer. What they won't tell you about is his mental instability, the fact he was used as a guinea pig by the CIA at such a young age. Wouldn't you want revenge on society if society treated you as he was treated? Rejected at every turn, misunderstood by so many to be a terrorist. The man just wanted to be understood; it was just that no one would listen. Defence rests."

With that, Ross went to sit down again with a smug smile on his face. Chloe stood up to counter.

"Wow! What a sob story. The fact of the matter is that this man is a terrorist. He is a killer, and whatever mental condition he may or may not have, it doesn't take away from the fact that he has killed people. He is guilty of this. Prosecution rests."

Chloe strutted back to her seat but not without sneaking a middle finger aimed at Ross. The two had been in competition since the beginning of school and always took an opportunity to get one over the other. The jury left to convene but rushed back within five minutes.

"We, the jury, find Ted Kaczynski guilty of first-degree murder and multiple counts of terrorism."

As the judge banged the gavel, Ross's head sank. He hated losing, even if it was a mock trial. He started to get up, but Jamal grabbed his arm.

"Where are you going?"

"Lunch."

"No, you cost us that. Now say sorry."

"Sorry, now bye."

Ross paced off, keeping his head down as he made his way to the canteen.

Luke sat cotched out in his room with the smoke as well as the stench of weed lingering in the air. He was blasting Juice WRLD's new album and sang along, slurring his words as his head felt as if it was among the clouds. The music cut out as his phone started to ring.

BILAL IS CALLING

"Yo, what you saying?" Luke answered.

"You good bro? Where you? I'm active in Harold Wood."

"I'm chilling at home bro. It'll take me a sec to get there. I'll take my mum's car – it's calm."

"*Aight bet… wait – ain't you frazzed?*"

"*Yeah and? You can drive high.*"

"*Bro – no you can't.*"

"*Shut up, you prick, yes you can. I'll bring some bud for you.*"

"*Aight calm, in a bit.*"

Luke put the phone down and stumbled up. He and Bilal had been friends for over six years. Bilal was two years above Luke but had taken a shine to him and saw him as his underling, his project. Since then, Luke had got involved in more and more illegal and questionable situations, becoming more out of control than Bilal ever was, so the dynamic of their friendship had changed.

Luke's eyes were burnt red and his head was spinning, but he managed to make it out of his room and down the stairs.

"*Yo Isobel. I'm taking your whip.*"

"*What? No Luke, you can't do that. You aren't even insured, and you're high!*"

"*Call the police then.*"

Luke slammed the door behind him and walked over to the gleaming, brand-new Mercedes-AMG parked down the street. He got into the driving seat and headed to Bilal's house.

After an hour's journey, Luke miraculously made it to Bilal's house and called him.

"*Bilal, I'm at your yard.*"

"*Aight, I'm coming. Oh, also my boy Jerome is here.*"

"*Bruv, what the fuck. I told you how I feel about new men.*"

"*He's calm, trust me.*"

"*Well, he ain't getting in the whip. Looks like we're walking.*"

"*Bro, Harold Wood is dead! There is nothing to do here.*"

"*Shut up, we're walking.*"

Luke slammed down the phone aggressively. He hated new people. Ever since he was young, he had always had a problem trusting people and building long-term commitments. He always kept his circle close and never told anyone the whole story about what was going on in his life as he never wanted it to be turned against him. He reached for the glove compartment and pulled out his bag and a small pocketknife, just in case. As he got out of the car, he saw Bilal and Jerome walking towards him.

"*Yo, this is my boy Jerome,*" Bilal stated.

"*Where you from?*" asked Luke.

"*Hackney, bruh, where you from?*" Jerome answered confidently.

"*Chelsea.*"

Jerome laughed.

"*Chelsea? You a posh boy, then! Probably bought that car with daddy's money.*"

Bilal took a step back.

"*Call me that again, I dare you.*"

"*Aight chill, posho, it was just a joke.*"

Luke pushed Jerome to the floor and got on top of him, pinning him down with a knee on his chest.

"*I don't react well to jokes.*"

"*Luke, chill bro, he was just kidding,*" Bilal bargained.

"*Bilal, shut the fuck up before I slit your throat.*"

Bilal took a further step back.

"*Now, you're going to apologise.*"

"*S-sorry man. Jesus Christ.*"

"*Good.*"

Luke moved his knee off his chest and stood up, extending a hand to Jerome, which he sheepishly accepted. Luke reached into his bag, and the others stepped back, alarmed. He pulled out a vacuum-sealed bag of weed.

"*Now we're all friends. Let's get high.*"

When Ross reached the canteen, he found it unusually empty for the start of lunch. He walked towards the till, picking up a single slice of pizza and a bottle of water. He never had much of an appetite and usually kept his diet simple. As he was about to pay, he heard a voice call his name.

"*Susie!*"

He turned around to see one of his few friends at school running towards him.

"*Hey Isaac, how are you doing?*"

Isaac was the most intelligent student at Harold Wood Grammar, having achieved all 9s at GCSE level and being on course for 5 A*s at A-Level. Isaac and Ross had despised each other throughout main school, but as sixth form started, they connected over a mutual hatred of the general school environment and the people in it.

"*I'm alright, man. I heard Dr Peters gave you a hard time again.*"

"*Yeah, he did. But it's fine. He's a prick, anyway.*"

"*Yeah, I guess.*"

"*Come, let's sit over there.*"

Ross and Isaac made their way to the corner of the canteen away from the commotion. The canteen began to fill up as they took their seats.

"*Look at them all,*" Ross said in disgust.

"*What do you mean, Sus?*"

"*Just like, they all walk in their little cliques and just sit and chat shit about their so-called friends all day and get into pointless relationships which just cause pain and listen to people who demand respect despite being rude and ignorant.*"

"*Are you ok, bro?*"

"*I'm going home.*"

Ross got up and made his way to the exit. The so-called "popular" group of boys walked past him, including Jamal. They all started bogging out Ross, staring at him as if he were a specimen in a museum. As he walked past, he accidentally bumped into Travis Cannon, the self-acclaimed most popular boy in the school.

"*Cuz, what the fuck!*" Travis exclaimed.

"*The fact that you use 'cuz' unironically clearly means this conversation is not worth my time.*"

"*Ooooo, look at me. I'm Ross Susans and I am smarter than everyone.*"

"*I am smarter than you. You use this ridiculous mask to hide how insecure you are, and your posy is no different. Now, goodbye.*"

"*You can say all you want, Sus, the fact of the matter is you aren't special. You're just like all of us. A poor cunt from Harold Wood going nowhere.*"

"*Yes, but unlike you, I am not going to stay here and be a bum my whole life.*"

"*What, like your brother?*"

Ross stopped in his tracks as Travis's posy began to snicker.

"*If you say anything about my brother again, I will end you.*"

"*Oh yeah? Hit me.*"

"*Violence is a fool's game. You're twice my size. I would be an idiot to pick a fight with you.*"

"*Yeah, that's what I thought, pussy. Now fuck off.*"

"*I would rather tell all your little followers about how your sister sent me nudes last week.*"

Travis' jaw hit the floor as his disciples started laughing. Ross walked away smoothly, holding his middle finger up.

"*Come back here you cunt!*"

Travis started running at Ross as he turned and sprinted off. He grabbed his bag off the floor and made a beeline for the school gate. The gate was open at lunch time, but it was now beginning to close as the clock struck 1:00. Ross was surprisingly quick for his build, but Travis was hot on his tail, screaming at him. As Ross got closer to the gate, his chances of success grew slimmer as it was closing at an alarming rate. He threw his bag through the gate and slid through as the gate shut behind him.

"*You prick! I'll kill you,*" Travis yelled.

"*They weren't all that, anyway!*" Ross replied confidently.

Ross strutted away as the victor. The truth of the matter was that Ross had no idea whether Travis even had a sister. If there was one thing he had learned in his life, it was how to read people and push people's buttons to get them to do what you want or get out of a sticky situation. He was a master of manipulation.

Ross knew his mum would be at work at lunchtime. The real reason he had left was not his distaste of the school, as great as that was, but to check on his brother. What the crackhead had said to him had been playing on his mind the entire day; he had to know the truth. Ross often skipped school. He viewed it as a place where people went to become workers, and as a creative thinker, he never thought like that. He wanted to try new things and experiment and felt that school only limited what he could do. He realised that he needed school to become the lawyer he'd always wanted to be, but he always promised himself he would do it his way, not relying on teachers or other students. He was convinced he could teach himself all the stuff, away from the pointless drama of secondary school.

As he was walking home, he heard a commotion on the other side of the street. A 6ft 2 lad had pinned another guy down to the ground with a fist about three inches away from his face, while another boy looked on like a coward. Ross always liked to analyse situations, and as he walked past and heard their indistinct screams, he thought, '*This, this is what I am trying to escape. I can't turn out like that.*" He swiftly moved on so as not to draw attention to himself; he had had enough encounters for one day.

As soon as he got home, he called out for his brother.

"Reece!"

There was no response.

"Reece! Where are you?"

Again, no response. He went to open his door, but it was locked.

"Reece, open the damn door!"

No response.

Ross was in a state of panic and began bashing the door. His efforts were fruitless until he took a step back and kicked the door down, forcing it off the hinges.

Reece lay on his bed unconscious and unresponsive. A pipe and glistening salt-like rocks lay at his side.

"Reece... Reece! Wake up!"

Ross started to shake as he picked up his phone and eventually managed to dial 999.

"Hello, hello. I need an ambulance... yes, it's my brother. I think he's overdosed... No, he isn't responsive. What did he do? Um, crystal meth, I think. I don't know for sure. Ok... thank you. Please hurry."

Ross crouched at his side and grabbed his hand. It was cold and pale.

"Reece, man, you told me you wouldn't ever do this hard shit. Come on, man, please talk to me."

Two sets of footsteps came up behind Ross.

Luke hit the first blunt for himself before passing the lighter to Jerome.

"You know what I love about weed?" Luke asked.

"What, bruv?"

"This shit just helps me escape. I don't have to worry about anything, and it ain't even bad for you."

"Alright, Einstein," Bilal chuckled.

"Rather be that than Mr 'I had to redo my GCSEs'."

Bilal went silent as Jerome burst out laughing.

"Yeah. Shut up, dumb cunt."

"Shut up, Jerome; ain't funny, Luke."

"Whatever."

The trio stood in a poorly lit alleyway smoking and listening to music. Luke chuffed his zoot quickly, like a professional, before putting it out on the floor.

"Yo, this some strong ass shit!" Jerome exclaimed.

"More where that came from, bruh," Luke said with a smile on his face.

Luke reached into his bag and pulled out 10 more vacuum-sealed packets of bud from his bag, all marked with the tag "**L.M.**".

"A tenner per pack," Luke stated.

"Luke, what the fuck? I didn't know you were a dealer!" said Bilal.

"I'm not a dealer, I'm a businessman," Luke argued.

"Bro, I'm sceptical about all this shit."

"Bilal, you're a fucking bitch. Do you want it or not?"

"Alright, give me two."

"That's what I thought, out here tryna be Mother Fucking Theresa."

"What about you, Jerome? Or are you also gonna turn into a fucking saint?"

"Yeah, I'll take four."

Luke went to hand over the six bags, but as he reached into his bag, he heard the faint sound of sirens blaring in the distance.

"Oh shit, fed!" yelped Bilal.

Luke turned to Jerome.

"Are you a fucking rat as well?"

The sirens grew closer, and Luke grew more anxious. Possession is one thing, but dealing comes with a lot more consequences. Luke turned to run, but at that moment an ambulance flashed by.

No police cars. Luke instantly calmed down and turned back to Bilal, smacking him on the head.

"You fucking donut, that wasn't fed."

"How was I supposed to know that?"

"Fucking idiot! Honestly, man, let's get out of here."

Ross turned around to see two women dressed in dark green paramedic uniforms. He rushed towards them, tears in his eyes.

"Please... please help him," he begged.

The two paramedics brushed past Ross, crouched down next to Reece and immediately got to work to try and save his life. Ross left the room; he was a brave boy, but even he couldn't bear to watch what could be his brother's final moments.

Reece was three years older than Ross and had a completely different story. Reece was born with autism and ADHD, making him an interesting and unique individual. He often took pride in his differences, but going to school with a group of insensitive and uneducated youths meant he was bullied to the point where he had to stop attending school. He dropped out at the age of 16, having previously wanted to go on and become a doctor, but his social circumstances limited him. He tried to find work, but without core qualifications, he found it difficult to hold anything down. He was left stranded and broke until work came and found him. He was walking home from Sainsbury's after an interview one evening and was approached by Harry "Crackhead" Smith. He convinced him he could make himself as much money as he desired, and Reece, desperate, agreed to take part in his work. Being only 17 at the time, he mainly did odd jobs for Harry, never fully knowing the details of the work he was doing, but the pay was enough for Reece not to question it. Harry had set up a very successful business model and was known around the area for his quality product, but this did not come without drawbacks. To ensure this product was always of the highest standard, Harry had a habit of testing his products not only on himself but also on his runners. He continued this trend with Reece, starting him with weed but slowly progressing to stronger substances including LSD, heroin and crystal meth. Reece had no option but to take the drugs or Harry would cut off his money supply, but he had no idea how addictive some of these drugs were. He was soon hooked. At the age of 19, Ross caught Reece snorting a line in the bathroom and immediately went and told their mother. Reece was put in rehab, and Ross had assumed he had recovered, but after a year he was still the same.

As Ross tried to process the situation in front of him, his mind raced back to what Travis had told him about his brother. He snapped out of the state he was in and marched next door.

He banged on the door of the crackhead, screaming every insult under the sun and causing a great commotion in all the flats around him. Despite his persistence, there was no answer, so he kicked the door down and burst in. The flat was empty. No sign of Harry or any of his deathly equipment, not even any furniture. Ross desperately started searching through what was left in the flat but found nothing. He was still searching when he heard familiar footsteps behind him.

"Excuse me, sir."

Ross turned to see one of the paramedics standing hesitantly behind him, looking distressed.

"What the fuck are you doing? Go help my brother!"

"Sir, you might want to sit down."

Shock hit Ross and he slumped to the ground. He didn't need the paramedic to say it, he knew. Reece was dead.

The trio walked down the street, all high as a kite with dainty red eyes, and stumbled through the bustling city centre.

"*Ain't this world crazy, man?*" Bilal exclaimed.

"*Shut your dumb ass up. None of that philosophical shit here, man.*"

"*Nah, but deep it, we exist. Like here, it's mad.*"

"*Shut the fuck up before I clart your dumb ass. Fucking imbecile fam. Talking about the point of life. Go pass your GCSEs first, you idiot.*"

"*I'm just saying, don't gotta be rude.*"

"*Fam, life is pointless. You live, you work, you die. Nothing else to it. Everyone is fake, and if people thought logistically, everyone should kill themselves.*"

"*That's some deep ass shit man – you ok?*"

"*Even if I wasn't, what you gonna do about it?*"

Bilal remained silent.

"*I'm dipping.*"

Luke spudded Bilal and bogged out Jerome before walking off back to his car. Luke was a very creative thinker. He was never afraid to speak his mind and was never afraid of other people's opinions of him. This was both an admirable quality and a dangerous one; he had no filter. As he was walking back to his car, his phone began to ring again.

Unknown Caller

Intrigued, Luke picked up but waited for the caller to speak.

"*Is this Luke Moffat?*"

"*Who's asking?*"

"*Callum… from the SD.*"

Luke paused. The SD were the biggest drug-running group operating around London. They got all their stuff imported from America and were so secret none of their members had ever been called in by police or caught. To stay secret, the name of the group changed depending on who was in charge, determined by the initials of a fake name chosen by the current boss. The SD were known for their violence. Despite being discreet, they were never afraid to raid other groups or use torture methods when necessary, which sometimes ended in murder.

"Yeah, what do you want?"

"We want to work with you, Luke."

"Work with what?"

"I'm not a fed. We've seen your packaging around. It's nice shit. We want to partner."

"No idea what you're on about."

"Listen, Luke. Either you help us and accept our partnership or we're going to have to take extreme measures."

"You think I'm scared of your threat? Come at me."

"No, no. I'm not talking about you. If you don't accept this, I will slit your sister's throat."

"What do you want me to do?"

"Get in the black car."

"Fucking nigga, there ain't a black car here!"

"Look across the street, you idiot. Oh, also if you're racist again I'll put a bullet through your head."

Callum hung up.

Luke looked over the road to see a blacked-out Mercedes with an ominous-looking bald man in the driving seat. He approached the car and took a seat in the back.

The car travelled around 20 miles with Luke and the driver sitting in silence before coming to a stop in the middle of an industrial estate.

"Get out."

Luke stepped swiftly out the car. He was met by a tall, large and menacing figure dressed in deep, stained black with slicked-back hair and thick sunglasses. He looked like a rockstar.

"*Luke Moffat?*" he enquired. Elegance in his voice.

"*Who are you?*"

"*I am the SD.*"

"*The SD is a group. This is fucking dumb, fam. All you with your faggot ass outfits acting like fucking movie stars.*"

"*What?*"

"*I said you act like a bunch of pussies.*"

"*I admire your arrogance.*"

"*Shut up man.*"

The man drew a gun from his waist and planted it against Luke's forehead, slamming his hand into his neck.

"*We work in a certain way around here so we don't get caught – do you understand?*"

"*Put me down, bruv.*"

"*When you learn some respect.*"

The man increased his grip on Luke's neck as his finger caressed the trigger, ready to fire at any given moment.

"*Alright man, fuck! Sorry.*"

"*Good.*"

The man released Luke's neck and removed the gun discreetly, putting it away before turning to Luke again.

"*I'm SD. Sean Davis. That's the only name you'll refer to me by. I've been leading the SD for the last five years. Before me, it was called JO, Jonathan Oluwa, and after me, it'll be some other dumb name. SD is just a way to keep it hidden.*"

"*Is it a rule for the leader to always be black?*" Luke chuckled to himself.

Sean took a step closer to Luke again.

"*Callum told me you were racist. Knock it off or I'll bury you in the ground, understand?*"

"*Understood, Captain!*"

"*If you didn't have potential, I would have buried you in the ground by now. But we can be business partners. Let's start with your product. Who's the supplier?*"

"*I grow it.*"

"*You grow it?*"

"*Yeah, in my shed. I've got a lab.*"

"*Alright, here's the deal. I can get your stuff all around London but only with SD packaging and I get some of the commission as well.*"

"*Fuck off. I work better on my own.*"

"*You really don't remember much, do you? It's either you do this, or Callum kills your sister, maybe does some other shit with her, I don't know. He's a weird guy.*"

"*You touch my sister, I'll take down your whole empire.*"

"*Doesn't need to get to that. Split 60/40 – you start getting me stuff by this evening.*"

"*One condition.*"

"*What's that?*"

"*You make me a partner at SD.*"

"*Partner? Bro, you are 18 years old.*"

"*Partner or no deal.*"

"*Fine, you're a partner. Get me that stuff by tonight or I'll come to your yard and collect it myself.*"

Sean walked off aimlessly into the industrial estate as Luke turned around and got back into the car that had brought him there.

7th January 2020

Ross stood in his flashy suit looking onto the murky field where his brother was to be buried. Ross hated wearing expensive suits, he thought it pretentious and condescending, but he made an exception today, the day of the funeral. It had taken Ross's family the better part of three months to arrange the funeral as they couldn't afford it. It was a tiny service with only around 30 people in attendance, many of whom didn't even know Reece. Ross stared down at the crumpled bit of paper in his hand. He had been asked to make a speech, knowing his mum didn't have the strength to do so.

"*It's time, son,*" his mum said gently to him.

Ross had always hated funerals. He didn't understand the concept of celebrating someone's life; he could only see the pain. He made his way to the rickety podium next to Reece's coffin. He paused to take a look at it before he began.

"*Reece was my brother. But he was more than that. He was my role model, my inspiration, my best friend. He was taken too early. I've experienced an abnormal amount of death in my short time, but I know Reece wouldn't want this to affect me to the point I quit. He wouldn't want it to stop any of us; we have to keep going. I made myself a promise after my father died and reaffirm that promise here. I said to Reece, 'I am going to be a lawyer,' and that's exactly what I plan to do.*"

Ross walked away from the podium into the arms of his mother. Really, he had made the speech more for himself than for those in attendance; he was on his own now. Just him and his mum. She embraced him with tears in her eyes. It was just the two of them against the world.

As Ross left the comforting embrace of his mother, he was approached by a man wearing a far more expensive suit than he was, with slicked-back hair and an aroma of lavender.

"*I'm sorry for your loss, Ross.*"

"Thank you… who are you?"

"My apologies, I'm Michael – I was good friends with your dad, and I knew your brother."

"Oh right, well thank you for your condolences."

Ross was going to move away but Michael stopped him.

"I heard you want to be a lawyer."

"Yeah, it's a goal of mine. What about it?"

"I have connections in America. I can refer you for the Harvard Award for you to go to study law there. I am an alumnus.

"Yeah, right. I'll be lucky if I can get into any law school."

"Ross, you can do this. Please think about it. The application is due in three weeks. If you decide to apply, I'll happily act as one of your references."

"What else would I need?"

"Not much. Your grades are already stellar; you would just need to write a personal statement."

"How am I even meant to trust you? I barely knew my dad."

"Ross, if there is one thing you can take from me it's that your dad was one of the best men to walk this earth. He loved you more than anything, even if it was from a distance. Go and make him proud."

"I'll think about it."

With that, Ross walked off. It was a tantalising offer, but he was wary. Harvard was one of the hardest schools to get into, let alone graduate from. It also meant leaving his mum behind, as well as his home, all he'd ever known, which he wasn't sure about doing.

When Ross arrived home from the funeral, he was shaken. The emptiness of the house hadn't really bothered him until today. It had set in that he had to take charge of his life. He sulked into his room, slamming down onto his bed. He opened his laptop and searched for the Harvard award application. The website stared him in the face as he contemplated starting his application. The summary read *"The Harvard Award is given to exceptional students found to have a talent in a particular field. These individuals will have come from various backgrounds but show a touch of class that can be used to expand their chosen field of study."* He was conflicted. Even if he got the award, it wouldn't cover the full cost of the tuition fees, so he would be putting even further strain on his mum, but this also gave him the opportunity to make sure his mum would never have to work a day in her life again. This latter thought motivated him to begin his application. Ross only wanted to help people; he never wanted anyone to experience the pain he had experienced and saw this as an opportunity to help others as well as himself. He opened up a word document and began typing up his statement.

Luke turned down a small side street in the heart of Hackney. He had been working for Sean Davis for the past three months, slowly establishing himself as a core member of the SD and quickly dismissing chatter about his quick rise to partner. Luke had started off as a general runner like the rest, but given his size and aggressive nature, he was more suited to the role of an enforcer. This meant that he was in charge of his own group of runners, but he would also sort out any tricky customers in his area and collect debts. Luke was currently en route to collect a debt. He approached a small set of flats just off Hackney city centre and went to ring the intercom. The woman he was after was Malake Maratunde, a serial offender who owed the SD over £5000 over the two years she had been buying from them to try and fund her heroin addiction. Sean had chosen to let her debt slide up to this point due to her age but had now had enough and sent Luke over to sort it out. Luke rang the bell for Flat 13.

    "… Hello?"

"*Postman, I have a parcel for you.*"

"*Leave it on the side.*"

"*It needs a signature.*"

"*Ok, two seconds.*"

Luke waited for the door to unlock, but after waiting for a minute he grew impatient and rang again. No answer.

In the distance, he heard a bump and a rustle in a bush before seeing Malake climbing out of a side window. He sprinted over. She managed to get out of the window and tried to run away, but Luke grabbed her arm and pulled her back to him.

"*Where do you think you're going, bitch?*"

"*I don't have any money!*"

"*Well, you have to pay your debt somehow.*"

"*How?*"

"*The stuff in your flat.*"

"*That isn't even mine! It's my son's!*"

"*Don't really care, love.*"

Luke dragged her by the wrist to the front of the building and forced her to open the door. As she was reaching into her purse to grab the key, Luke gripped her by the shoulder to make sure she didn't run off.

She finally found her key and handed it to Luke. As Luke went to unlock the door, he heard words coming from behind.

"*What the fuck do you think you're doing?*"

Luke spun around to see Jerome standing with a look of disgust and confusion on his face.

"*Get the fuck away from my mum.*"

"*Your mum is in debt.*"

"*Bro, what are you playing at? Wait until I tell Bilal about this shit.*"

"Bilal won't do shit, and neither will you. Now fuck off, cunt."

"No, let her go. Now!"

Luke threw Malake to the ground and squared up to Jerome, getting in his face.

"What are you gonna do about it? I never liked you – seems like being a prick is in the family."

"Say that again."

"Your mum is a fucking junkie."

Jerome lashed out, pushing Luke to the floor before getting on top of him and landing a solid blow to his chest. Luke felt the blow but used his superior frame to overpower Jerome, switching him onto the floor and landing three consecutive blows to his abdominal region before pinning his neck down.

"Now. Either I choke you out and then batter your mum the same. Or you let me take the stuff from the flat and any money you have on you."

"You think you're hard. Wait until my brother hears about this. You'll be dead! You're just a rich bitch tryna be something he ain't."

Luke slammed down harder on his neck.

"I'll do your brother the same as you, and any other prick you send."

Luke held Jerome's gaze, and he eventually gave in, giving over his wallet as well as his car keys.

"Smart man."

Luke relaxed his grip on Jerome and stood up.

"Just one more thing."

Luke reached into his waist and pulled out a pistol, firing without warning into Jerome's forehead. Jerome's mum let out a scream as his body slumped lifelessly to the ground.

"I'd say that debt's paid off. Don't fuck with us again."

Ross stared blankly at his screen as his mind processed what he had typed. He became more and more displeased with what he had written. He deleted the word document and slammed his laptop down on the floor. It was never wise to attempt such an important task on a day as emotional as it had been today, but Ross was never one to stay down. He knew life never threw any luck his way. He liked it like that, the challenge. He heard a knock on his door, and his mum came in.

"You ok? I heard a bang."

"Yeah, fine. Was just trying to do some work."

"The Harvard thing?"

"Yeah. I just don't know if it's the best thing to do."

"Ross… it's Harvard! It's the best school in the world for law."

"But it would mean leaving here… leaving you."

His mum moved closer. *"Ross, you have to go live your life."*

"But –"

"But nothing. There is nothing here for you. You saw what happened to Reece. You have a chance here. A chance to go and do something for the world. I've lived my life. The thing that would make me happiest is if you lived a better life than I was able to give you."

Ross's eyes welled up with tears again as he collapsed into his mother's arms. Life had never been fair to him, but it had been even harsher on her, left to raise two boys on her own with no support other than occasional child benefits and a part-time cleaning job. She was Ross's hero and inspiration.

"I've gotta go, Mum."

"Go? Where?"

"Don't worry about that. I'll be back for dinner. We'll watch a film together."

"Ok son, don't be too late. Be safe, please."

"Always."

As day turned into night, Ross prepared to leave the house, throwing on his jet-black jacket and worn-out air forces. Despite what he had been through, he was still a teenager. His intentions tonight were far from pure, however. He was on a hunt. For Harry Smith.

Ross exited the flat to the sound of light rain. He made a move for the stairs after checking the flat next door one last time. Still no sign of anyone and a broken door to top it off. Harry's runners always used to chill down below the estate at the kid's park, baiting youngers to expand their hold on the estate, all addicted to different drugs as test subjects for Harry. As he got to the bottom of the stairs, he was surprised to see a familiar face approach him. It was Isaac.

"Susie!" he exclaimed.

"Hey man, what's up?"

"Nothing man. Thought I'd come and check on you after today especially."

"Thank you, bro, it means a lot. I'm good."

"Where are you going?"

"To get a gun."

"A gun? What the fuck is wrong with you? I thought you were good!"

"Yeah, I'll be fine after I blow that sick fuck to hell."

"Who?"

"You know man, the crackhead."

"Bro."

"Don't try and talk me out of it."

"He killed himself."

Ross paused.

"After what happened to Reece, I think he realised what he had done. Or he just overdosed. That guy was fucking mental."

"Yeah. Deserved, though."

"You were gonna get a gun – you're funny, you know. What was your clown ass gonna do with a gun?" Isaac laughed.

"Shut up man."

"Where were you gonna get it anyway?"

"Them lot over there."

Ross signalled to the group of youths at the gate of the kids' block.

"They're dangerous, man."

"Yeah, no shit. Let's get out of here, get something to eat."

As Ross led the way out of the estate with Isaac close behind him, they heard two loud gunshots followed by screaming and footsteps fleeing the scene.

"What the fuck?"

"What the fuck is wrong with you, Luke? The job was to intimidate, not fucking kill a man!"

"Bruv, you fucking said go deal with it. So, I fucking dealt with it."

"This is the third person you've killed in three fucking months!"

"Yeah, consistency innit."

Sean slammed the table.

"Listen, you cocky shit. You don't play smart with me. I am bigger than you, I am smarter than you and I'll deal with you if I have to."

"Everyone is shaking!"

Sean grabbed a knife off the table and slashed Luke's finger. Luke screamed in anger.

"I told you. You do things how I want them done. That way, we don't get caught."

"Fine, fucking prick."

Sean sat back in his chair. They were sat in one of his offices that had been cleared out for a business conference. He was a very successful businessman and a respected member of the community.

The perfect cover to run an international drug business. His expensive suit stood in stark contrast to Luke's Givenchy tracksuit.

"Learn to dress better as well, yeah."

"Suck my dick."

Sean was about to get riled up again as Callum burst through the door.

"Yo, fam," he started.

"What, bruv?" Luke replied.

"The fucking crackhead. He killed himself."

"Nah, can't be true. You're standing right in front of me." Luke chuckled to himself.

"Shut up, you cretin."

"Fuck sake!" Sean exclaimed while banging on the desk again.

"You're gonna break that thing, you know."

"Not. Another. Word."

"What we gonna do, bruv?"

"Who the fuck is the crackhead?"

"Harry Smith, ran Waterside Estate, Harold Wood."

"Who cares about Harold fucking Wood?"

"The fucking Vayans man. They'll take that area."

"Vayans? Do you all have faggot ass names?"

"Luke. You're gonna go sort this."

"Him? What the fuck, blud?"

"Yo, Callum. By the way. It's 2020. No one under the age of 40 uses blud."

"See what I fucking mean!"

"Luke, shut up. You and Callum are gonna go together and sort this out."

"What are we meant to do?"

"Go over there and chat to Harry's old runners. Callum knows the usuals. If there are any new men, just let them know that it's still our turf and everything goes through us.

"Easy as."

"Luke. No more killing."

Luke made an ironic salute as he got up out of the office chair and walked to the doorway where Callum was waiting. The two exited the building surrounded by flashy suits and the smell of out-of-date coffee. The urgency of all the workers in the building made Luke and Callum invisible as they quickly moved down the building and into the fabulous setting of Central London.

"Where the fuck is Harold Wood?"

"Follow me, cuz," replied Callum.

"Why do you speak like some 1950s roadman?"

"Shut the fuck up. We've gotta get the train, come."

The pair made their way to Waterloo station just over the road, progressed through the equally packed train station and after two stops arrived at Harold Wood.

"Take this, man." Callum offered Luke a mask.

"Why do I need a mask?"

"They don't know you. They won't trust you."

"So, what the fuck is a mask gonna do about that?"

"I'm gonna say you're my boy, Yanizi. You look like him."

"And where the fuck is Yanizi?"

"Dead."

"All you fucking men end up dead, bruv."

"Come, we're here."

The pair followed the signs to the exit. Waterside estate sat overlooking the station, one of the most run-down estates in the city. The council saw it as a lost cause and never tried to improve it. The pair turned out the station and down toward the estate.

"You got your strap?"

"Always."

They progressed down the poorly lit road, their steps echoing around the empty street as the rain trickled down. At the entrance to the estate was a short field with a playground situated in the centre of it, a prime place for drug movement after sunset. As Callum and Luke approached, a group of shadows turned their heads in unison. Harry Smith's runners were not like other runners. They weren't just kids that wanted to make money; they were smart and well-trained as men of the road but also businessmen and women. Callum and Luke continued confidently through the muddy field, the squelching noises making the situation somehow even more tense.

"*Stop there, bruv,*" one of the shadows called out.

"*It's Callum.*"

"*Callum who?*"

"*Callum from SD.*"

"*And who's that?*"

"*Yanizi.*"

"*Why ain't he speaking then?*"

"*I don't like to waste my breath.*"

"*Alright, what do you want?*"

"*Just come to see how the situation is since Crackhead died.*"

"*Crackhead was an idiot. Tried to get us all hooked on drugs. Reece was the only one who fell for that stupid shit.*"

"*Yeah, he was. But wagwan now, though.*"

Luke started laughing.

"*Waaaaag-wannnnnn.*"

"*Shut up, you idiot,*" Callum muttered.

"*Ayo, ain't Yanizi dead?*" another shadow exclaimed, a girl this time.

Callum paused.

"*Answer her then!*"

"*Nah, I'm right here, bruv. You can see my dick if you want.*"

"*That ain't Yanizi, bruv.*"

"*Aight, look, calm down. This is Luke, he works for the SD now.*"

Luke pulled down his mask to reveal a smiling face.

"*Why you smiling, bruv?*"

"*I've got a question for you.*"

"*What's that?*"

"*Who do you sell for?*"

Luke took a step closer to the shadows. He made out three of them upon closer inspection.

"*No one, bruv. Waterside is its own thing. SD has always respected that.*"

"*What about the Vayans?*"

The shadows fell silent.

"*Well?*"

"*Yeah, we get some of our stuff from them, now.*"

"*Ah. So, we do have an issue.*"

"*Nah, you've got a problem. Fucking pussyole.*"

"*Do you know what my name is?*"

"*Lawrence or some shit.*" The shadows started to chuckle.

Luke reached for his waist, revealing his Glock before firing two shots at the legs of the shadow standing closest to him. The other two took a step back, screaming.

"*What the fuck, bruv!*" the man spluttered, desperately trying to stop the blood flowing out of his legs. Luke got his torch out and shined it at him. Lying on the floor, covered in blood, was a young man, 22 at the most, with a thick beard, dark complexion, a tattoo on his right arm and now two bullet holes in his knees.

"*Name?*"

"*Terence.*"

"*Alright, well now you're gonna be called handicapped. Cause you're a fucking cripple.*"

"*What do you want, man?*" Terence said, shaking in shock.

"Oi, you two cunts listen up as well. Unless you wanna end up like this. You sell our food and our food only. If the Vayans ask why you ain't moving theirs, you come to me. And you tell everyone that Luke fucking Moffat did this to you. Understand?"

"Yes fam, yes! Just help me, please."

"Help your bredrin fam."

Luke allowed the other two shadows to come forward, a girl no older than 18 and another young male no older than 15. They helped Terence up and carried him into the estate. Luke turned to Callum.

"Easy as."

"What did Sean fucking say, bruv?"

"He said don't kill him. So, I crippled him."

"I had a good relationship with these guys. Why do you have to be so aggressive?"

"See you, yeah Callum. Me and you are very different individuals. People don't respect kindness. People respect authority. Fear orders people; it controls people. I wouldn't expect you to understand. You're dumb and you're soft."

"Fucking Shakespeare out here."

"I'd rather be Shakespeare than your dumb ass."

"Yo bruv."

Callum pointed over to two kids staring at Callum and Luke.

"What the fuck are they looking at?"

Luke stormed over to the kids, who grew taller as he got closer to them until he realised they were his age. The teenagers didn't move as Luke approached.

"Oi, fucking dickheads."

The teenagers still stood in silence.

"Respond to me when I fucking talk to you."

"My mum told me never to talk to strangers!" one called out.

"Fucking joke, man. Ok, then."

For the second time that evening, Luke reached to his waist, pulling out his strap and aiming at the teenagers. That got their attention and the two dispersed instantly, sprinting off round the back of the estate but not before Luke got a shot off, narrowly missing both of them. Callum rushed up behind Luke and took him down to the ground before taking his gun off him and slapping him across the face.

"*What's wrong with you, man? They're kids! One was in school uniform, for fuck sake!*" *he screamed.*

"*Witnesses.*"

"*You're too trigger happy. The aim is not to get caught, you idiot.*"

The pair turned their heads as they heard sirens closing in from various angles.

"*Fucking fed man, let's go.*"

"*What the fuck was that Ross?*" screamed Isaac in panic.

"*Shush man, just keep quiet.*"

"*We have to go, now!*"

Ross ignored Isaac's advice. He was always naturally curious about everything around him and had a specific interest in this event. Even he was unsure why, which piqued his interest even more. Ross spotted a figure slowly making its way towards them. He chose to ignore the impending threat, just trying to work out who was approaching them.

"*Let's get out of here!*"

"*Wait.*"

Ross insisted on waiting for the figure to get closer. He was intrigued, attracted by danger. Ross never feared death. The figure shouted something, but Ross couldn't work out what he was saying so he stood his ground waiting for further information.

"Respond to me when I fucking talk to you!" the figure called out.

"My mum said not to talk to strangers!"

The figure came closer to reveal a tall, built individual with black hair and a menacing stare. He couldn't make out his face entirely. He muttered something to himself before reaching to his waist, pulling out a gun and firing a few shots towards Ross and Isaac. The pair dashed away, with the shots narrowly missing them, before they eventually stopped after another figure tackled the man to the ground.

"Let's go, man!"

Isaac and Ross rushed off round the back of the estate and out to the high street as the sound of sirens began to close in.

"What the fuck is wrong with you man? Why didn't we just run?"

"Thought I recognised him."

"Nah, trust me, we've never seen him before; he was mammoth."

"Yeah, I guess. Come, let's get something to eat."

The pair trudged through the dimly lit high street to the local chicken shop, both visibly shaken by what had just occurred. They ordered 10 wings to split between them and a portion of chips to go with it, totalling £5.99. They took a seat at one of the two tables the chicken shop offered and sat in near silence while they ate, both too upset to say a word. The situation was tense and grew tenser as three policemen entered the shop, laughing and joking. Isaac and Ross froze but were careful not to make eye contact with the officers to avoid conversation. The policemen ordered their meals and took a seat at the table opposite Ross and Isaac, almost forcing them to look at them. Every time one of their radios went off, Ross and Isaac tensed up. They had done nothing wrong, but given both their family situations and where they were from, it was more than likely they would be blamed, and no one would be too bothered. The radio continued to go off as Isaac had the last wing and Ross downed his drink. Ross signalled to Isaac to get up, and they casually left the chicken shop, being mindful not to pay too much attention to the officers to avoid suspicion.

After a 20-minute walk spent mostly listening to music to avoid any awkward conversation, the pair reached Isaac's house. Isaac lived perhaps one of the most average lives an individual could live. His dad worked for the council, and his mum was a teacher, and they lived in a standard neighbourhood where all the houses look the same. He was also destined to live this type of life, despite being intelligent beyond belief. His dream was to take on a similar role to his dad as his hero. Ross could not stand to live this kind of life. Although comfortable, he found it boring repeating the same monotonous schedule with only two weeks off a year; he desired more. Isaac spudded Ross before going home as his sister opened the door. Ross gave her a wave and walked off.

Ross began the 20-minute journey back from Isaac's to the estate, as he had done so often over his school years. His mind began to wander as he walked back. He couldn't stop thinking about the man who had shot at him. He appeared so familiar yet so distant, and his energy seemed drawn to him for reasons he couldn't quite understand. His attention was diverted back to the pavement as another one of his favourite songs came on – In my Room by Frank Ocean. Ross had a special appreciation for music. It was his escape. He listened to it 24/7 in an attempt to express or explain his feelings. Certain songs carried a lot of weight for Ross, and he loved the release of emotion it brought him. Given the events which had just occurred, Ross completely forgot about his brother. Processing this kind of emotion is almost impossible. Grief never leaves, especially when affecting those so young. It stays like a shadow, seemingly not visible most of the time but then coming out when you think the sun is shining brightest. Ross let himself feel the music as he continued down the wet, dark path. However, he wasn't scared. Despite all his surroundings being those which are most likely to scare an individual, he trudged on without a care in the world, focusing on nothing but his music.

Ross's mind was still firing various thoughts about the day he'd had. He had buried his brother and almost been buried himself on the same day. He homed in on this thought, specifically. He realised what he'd actually planned to do and how he could have died if things had been slightly different. His thoughts then wandered to his mum, and this really put things in perspective for Ross. The life that he could so easily live would only end in pain. Society's expectation of Ross was that he would become a murderer or a dealer or even a rapist, and because this was their expectation, no one would say much about the situation. Ross wanted to break the cycle. He wanted to make it out, but not through the road, through applying himself and making it without any consequences or threats hanging over his head. These thoughts continued to motivate him as he got back to Waterside. He was going to make it.

Luke and Callum caught their breath at the station after sprinting away from the estate. They passed through the station quickly but silently to avoid suspicion. They made it onto the train back to Chelsea, stopping at Waterloo to meet with Sean. As the first few stops passed, the train carriage cleared out and Callum turned to Luke.

"What the hell is wrong with you?"

"You still on about this? I dealt with it."

"No, you think you can just go about like this is your business."

"Business? Grow up man, you're a glorified runner."

"You need to learn respect."

Callum moved his face closer.

"Get out my face, you 40-year-old freak."

As tensions continued to rise, Callum's phone rang.

SD IS CALLING

"Yeah, boss?"

Luke couldn't overhear their conversation, nor was he interested in it. He had become more and more frustrated with Sean and Callum and believed he was better suited than both of them to running the SD. The pair had a five-minute conversation while Luke plugged his AirPods in and hit shuffle on his playlist. On came Know Me by NAV – Luke's favourite artist. Luke idolised his kind of life: drugs, women, money and violence. He never understood the human desire to follow all the rules and act with kindness; he had never known kindness to be rewarding in a world that had always been cruel to him. Luke had become engrossed in the song as Callum ended his conversation with Sean.

"Change of plan. I've gotta go deal with something. You meet Sean. I'll meet you later."

"Whatever, man."

"In a bit."

"Why you acting so weird bruv?"

Luke stared at Callum in confusion as he sheepishly got up and exited at the next stop. Luke tried to think about what Callum would have to go deal with but came to the conclusion that it wasn't about Callum; Sean wanted to see him. He became excited at the thought of Sean finally seeing he could be on the same level as him. The train continued on its way through Central London, eventually arriving at Waterloo where Luke departed. He made his way past the milling crowd toward Sean's building. He entered the building and went to the elevators to go up to Sean's floor. As he made his way through the foyer, he was surprised to be stopped by security at the elevators.

"What the fuck bruv?"

"Who are you here to see, boy?"

"*Don't boy me.*"

The elevator let off a ding as Sean stepped out, instantly alarmed to see Luke in front of him. He stepped between the security guard and Luke to stop the confrontation and explained to the security guard how Luke had reached out to him for mentorship in the stock market. The security guard seemed sceptical but eventually decided to let the pair go after checking Sean's ID. Sean gripped Luke by the shoulder and swivelled him round before marching out of the building. As they stepped out, Sean dragged Luke round a corner before slapping him on the head.

"*I told you before, ring me when you're outside.*"

"*Sorry bruv, I forgot. What did you want to talk about?*"

"*Have you got blood on your shoes? Jesus Christ, Luke.*"

Luke looked down, and sure enough, his Air Max 95s were covered in blood splatters from when he had shot Terence in the leg. He quickly took them off and threw them into the nearest garbage disposal.

"*Did you kill him?*"

"*Nah, crippled.*"

"*Luke, for fuck sake!*" Sean yelled.

"*I fucking dealt with it! What's this about anyway?*"

"*Fuck sake! Anyway, at least he's alive. I've got something to tell you.*"

"*Finally.*"

"*I wanna make you a CEO in SD, alongside me.*"

Luke couldn't help but release a smile. He thought he had deserved this from the start and now grew a little fonder of Sean for understanding they were on the same level.

"*Fucking finally – took you a while!*"

"*A few things...*"

"*You know, seeing as I should have had this from the start.*"

"*Luke!*" Sean snapped.

Luke straightened up in shock and turned to face Sean, now listening intently.

"*A few things. First, you have to stop swearing in every sentence. Second, dress nicer and finally, stop shooting people.*"

"*Two out of three. We'll call it even.*"

"*I can't have you killing people as my equal.*"

"*I didn't mean that, partner. I ain't stopping swearing. I'll happily do it in a suit.*"

Sean shook his head as Luke let out a wry laugh. Sean looked down at his phone as he got a notification.

"*That's Callum. I've gotta go meet him.*"

"*Aight calm, I ain't been home all day anyway.*"

"*Oh, and Luke.*"

Luke paused and turned around.

"*Yeah?*"

"*This life you're choosing, it doesn't come without consequences and sacrifices.*"

"*Done you alright innit.*"

Sean took one more look at Luke, nodding, before walking down the alley toward the other side of the street. Luke turned away, ecstatic at what he had just been told. He was finally in the big time. He wasn't just a shotter anymore or a thug; he had the potential to become a real businessman. As Luke walked back to the station, Sean's last words went through his head. He knew this life wasn't easy, nor would it bring much success without sacrifice. Luke quickly dismissed the doubt that entered his head and remembered that he was the only one that mattered. Oher people's lives rarely mattered to Luke. He had so much built-up anger and such a mix of emotions, and he had never been taught how to deal with the explosion within his head. He spent the rest of the train journey back to Chelsea trying to make sense of what he was thinking but didn't manage to grasp any of it, so he stuck his music on, this time listening to Dutchavelli – Bando Diaries. Luke relaxed back in his seat and let the music shuffle for his hour-long journey.

Eventually he arrived at Fulham Broadway station, right next to Stamford Bridge and his house. Luke stared at Stamford Bridge as he stepped off the train. Hee used to have aspirations of becoming a footballer but gave it up early after losing motivation to even attend training regularly. He became lost in thought as he made it round the corner and walked down his street. He took out his AirPods and looked down at his phone. He had a voicemail from Callum, but he couldn't be bothered to deal with his nonsense, so he left it for tomorrow.

Luke approached his front door; something was off. He did a full 360, feeling like he was being watched. He paused another second before opening his grand door. Luke was surprised to see the front light off and the alarm switch turned off.

"Yo, Isobel!"

Luke called a few times for his mum and Georgia to no response. Every light in the house was off. Luke grew more suspicious by the second and carefully made his way through the living room. He was halfway through the entrance when he heard a thud upstairs. Luke turned sharply toward the staircase, drawing his gun. He carefully progressed up the glass staircase, being careful not to make a sound. The thudding continued until it turned into a voice. It was Georgia.

"Luke... Luke!"

Luke sprinted up the stairs and slammed the locked door open. His eyes took a second to adjust to the light, but when they did, he was shocked by what he saw. Georgia lay in her bed, beaten and tied to the sides of the bed, tears streaming from her eyes.

"Georgia, what the fuck happened?"

"Someone came in… I heard Mum scream downstairs, and then he came upstairs. He had a gun and tied me to the bed…"

"Yes? And?"

"He raped me."

Luke's expression went from horror to outrage. He may have thought he cared only about himself, but his anger here was so high even he could not argue he cared for his sister.

"Who was it?"

"He said he left you a voicemail."

Georgia continued to sob as Luke untied her and gave her a careful hug, aware of her bruises. Luke pulled out his phone and dialled the voicemail left by Callum.

"Ah, Luke! I see you've found my little surprise. Don't worry, I was gentle."

Callum laughed on the phone, and Luke threw his hand into a wall, ripping apart the plaster.

"This is what Sean meant by consequences and sacrifices. We all have to deal with them in this business. This is a reminder to you that you aren't the dog's bollocks, you're ours. We own you. Hopefully, now, you'll learn respect."

That was the end of the voicemail, but Luke noticed Callum had also left a second one.

"Oh, and you might wanna check the kitchen, 'cuz'."

That was the end of the second message, sending Georgia into an instant panic. Still in tears, she jumped up, frantically shouting at Luke, asking him what he had done. Luke sat motionless; his mind was roaring with anger, but his reaction was bland. He got away from Georgia's grasp and rushed downstairs to the kitchen.

He switched the light on and walked into a blood bath. His mum sat motionless in a chair, a single bullet hole in her forehead. Georgia followed Luke and grabbed her phone to dial 999. Luke threw on his jacket again and dialled Callum's number while rushing out of the house. The phone kept ringing. Luke dialled Sean. Still no answer. In a rage, he examined his contact list; he knew that Callum lived near Stratford in a flat on an estate called Yale Valley. He called Bilal.

"*What, bruv? It's like midnight.*"

"*Get up, now. Meet me at Stratford. Bring your piece.*"

"*Why, fam?*"

"*Stop asking fucking questions. Come now!*"

"*Ok, ok. I'm coming. I'll be 30.*"

"*Hurry up.*"

Luke hung up. He sprinted down his street and made his way to Fulham Broadway station. He jumped on the final train to Stratford, not worrying about how he would get back. He heard the faint sound of sirens as his train left the station.

Within 20 minutes, Luke arrived at Stratford and met up with Bilal at the entrance. He was standing in the cold with his arms outstretched in confusion.

"*Why the fuck am I here, fam?*"

"*Just follow me.*"

"*Nah man, first you kill Trevor and now you randomly call me telling me to meet you here with a fucking gun.*"

"*Enough fucking questions man. Come!*"

"*Nah bruv.*"

Luke gripped Bilal by his neck and slammed him against the wall, knocking the wind out of him before landing a kick to his stomach.

"*Someone's just killed my mum and raped my sister. Now if you're done, I'm gonna blow his brains out.*"

"*Fucking hell man.*"

"*Are you coming or not?*"

Bilal stayed silent. Luke took this as his answer and stormed off, but Bilal called out behind him.

"You're a madman, you know."
Luke stopped.
"No bro, I'm a real man."

Luke turned away, ignoring Bilal's multiple calls to stop him. He didn't have the energy to chase Luke as he dissolved into the shadows.

Luke set his course for Yale Valley Estate, Flat 156. He walked the two miles to the estate, music blasting out of his AirPods as he tried to contain his anger. He pulled out his mask as he approached the bottom of the estate where a few smokers were lounging, blocking the entrance to the stairs. Luke didn't pay too much attention to them as he tried to make his way up the stairs, but an outstretched arm stopped him.

"Woah, woah. Where do you think you're going, son?"

Without hesitation, Luke drew his gun and smacked the man in the head, knocking him to the ground. He didn't want to shoot him and attract attention. He glared at the other three smokers.

"Fuck off."

The group quickly dispersed, leaving their friend lying still on the pavement. Luke made his way up the stairs to the third floor. He paused at the top of the stairs to catch himself and get his emotions under control.

Callum sat holding his three-year-old daughter on his lap while his wife in the kitchen cooked dinner. He smiled as he held the love of his life in his arms, admiring every inch of her before kissing her on the forehead. There was a knock on the door. Callum got up to answer it, but his wife insisted on getting it. She opened the door and screamed. Her body hit the ground as Luke barged in. Callum panicked and hid his daughter behind him. Luke made his way through the flat until he found Callum and his daughter in the living room.

"Cute daughter. Does she know her dad's a rapist?"

"Fuck off, Luke. Your issue is with Sean, not me. He instructed me."

Luke sarcastically nodded his head a few times, ironically smiling before looking Callum dead in the eye. He flipped the table in front of him, prompting tears from Callum's daughter. Luke drew the gun from his waist, fixing his aim at Callum's heart.

"You sick, sick man."

Callum began to shake as his words came out as splutters. Luke took a step closer and sat next to Callum, planting his gun firmly on his neck.

"You killed my mum and raped my sister. I have to deal with that. And now you'll have to deal with this," Luke whispered.

Luke fired two shots into Callum's neck and his body collapsed to the floor, blood staining the carpet and the cries of Callum's daughter filling the room. Luke tucked the gun away, unfazed, before spitting on Callum's body. He turned to his daughter.

"It's ok darling, your dad was a horrible man."

As Luke was about to leave, he pulled his mask down and glanced at the daughter. A wave of compassion come over him, and he went back and kneeled beside her.

"I'm sorry you had to see that. I'll come back for you. I promise."

With that, Luke left the apartment, closing the door behind him as if nothing had happened. He didn't need to worry about police. Everyone on this estate participated in illegal activities, so no one wanted the police anywhere near it. He walked calmly down the stairs, dialling Sean's number. His phone went to voicemail again, so he left him one.

"Sean. I'm coming for you."

23rd August 2020

Ross had been awake all night, tossing and turning. Today was A-Level Results day. Ross had never been good with anticipation; he always got incredibly nervous and often wouldn't sleep or eat for days. However, the day had finally arrived, the day that would predict his future. Not only was it A-Level Results day, but it also was the day Ross would hear back from Harvard on his application. Ross rolled across his bed for about the fiftieth time and reached for his phone. He had been conversing with Isaac all night, both worried about what might be ahead. Isaac had applied to Oxford and set his sights on becoming a professor in some sort of literature. The pair were currently talking about the possibility of Ross moving away and how big an opportunity it could be for him. Ross was deeply engrossed in the conversation until he acknowledged the time. It was 8:59, one minute till the results and the Harvard Award were emailed to him.

As the clock struck 9:00, the pair threw their phones down before reaching for their laptops and opening up their emails. Ross was shaking as he saw the notifications pop up on the side of the screen, first the results followed by the Harvard award. Ross's phone began to ring as he was about to click on the email. Isaac was calling.

"I fucking did it! I got into Oxford!"

Isaac was ripe with jubilation, and Ross was happy for him. He deserved it after the hard work he had put in across the seven years at school. Isaac continued to scream as Ross stared into his screen.

"One second, I'm gonna go tell my parents," and he rushed off. Ross took a deep breath and opened the first email, the A-Level Results email. He confirmed his details before scrolling down to the attachment. He took another deep breath before opening it; his

future lay waiting. He clicked on it and stared at it for a moment before starting to cry – tears of joy. There were two A*'s and two A's. He smiled as the tears streamed down his face. Isaac called again, but Ross chose to ignore him to allow himself to experience this on his own, just for a moment.

His moment was interrupted by his mum strolling in after hearing his conversation. He welcomed this interruption, softly embracing her and explaining the grades he had got. She also broke down in tears and told him how proud of him she was, especially after everything he had been through. The two hugged in silence for a while before Ross whispered into his mum's ear.

"*Thank you… for everything.*"

"*This is only the beginning for you. What about Harvard?*"

In all the excitement, Ross had completely forgotten about the second email. He leapt back to his computer and paused again, taking a deep breath before opening the email, this time with his mother's arm around his shoulder. He opened the email. Ross looked his mum in the eyes.

"*What? Did you get in?*"

"*I'm going to Harvard, Mum.*"

The two broke down again. It had been an emotional year for them, and this was the break they had been waiting for. They embraced each other once again and stayed in the comfort of each other's arms for a few minutes until Ross's phone rang again.

"*That's Isaac again. I should probably pick up.*"

"*Of course. I love you, and I'm so proud of you.*"

Ross gave his mum one final hug before picking up the phone.

"*Ross! Bro, how did it go?*"

"*I got in bro.*"

Isaac let out a whoop of joy. The pair had really had only each other through school, and to see each other succeed in the way that they had was wonderful. After Isaac calmed down, they discussed what they were going to do to celebrate later, including having a drink in a field, the classic way. Ross grinned. He couldn't remember the last time he had smiled for real. Everything that had happened had brought a true sense of relief; he was finally going to make it out.

Isaac continued to ramble on, projecting their future, as Ross stayed present in the moment. He looked up at his ceiling and closed his eyes, reaching out for Reece. In the midst of all the emotion, he found a moment of peace with his brother.

"Ross you wanker!"

Ross snapped back to reality and returned to the conversation.

"Yes bro, sorry."

"Are we going then?"

"Where?"

"You never listen, do you? Meet me at mine, you smart cunt."

Ross laughed as Isaac hung up and got ready to go out. He kissed his mum goodbye and left the flat.

Luke sat confidently on the local park bench with a cigarette planted firmly between his fingers. His dark tracksuit matched the environment perfectly, mirroring the murky day that lay ahead. He lit the cigarette and exhaled with relief. He felt the tuft of hair on his chin that could not even be called a beard and put his head down. He drew another puff of the cigarette as he stared down the hill. Students were running around, some with joy and some with disappointment. For a second, he thought about the fact that this would have been his results day as well. He dismissed this thought as his phone started to ring.

"Yo."

"Who's this bruv?"

"Bilal."

"Why you calling me on No caller, you donut?"

"You said so… never mind. I found him."

"Who?"

"Sean."

Luke took another puff. He had been hunting Sean for the better part of a year, but the man was a ghost. He had even put a hit out on him and interrogated some other members of the SD, which lead to nothing, but it seemed he finally had a breakthrough.

"Are you fucking sure? Don't fuck with me, Bilal."

"Yes fam, I literally just saw him go in this yard. I'll text you the address."

"Aight, meet me there in 10 minutes."

"I'm already here bruv."

"Shut up."

Luke hung up the phone and leapt up off the bench, throwing his lighter in his pocket. He jogged down the hill and checked the text he had received from Bilal; the address was in Mitcham, and Luke hopped on the train directly there.

After the short train journey, Luke rang up an old school friend, Mikaeel, who had moved away and now lived in Mitcham. Mikaeel was an even bigger troublemaker than Luke back at school and had been expelled from their school in Chelsea, which coincided with his parents' decision to move to Mitcham. Luke hadn't seen Mikaeel in two years but had heard that he lived much the same lifestyle as before, even more so now he was in Mitcham.

"Yo bruv."

"What you saying, who's this?"

"Luke, from school."

"I don't know no Luke."

"From Chelsea."

"No way! Luke Moffat?"
"Yeah bruv."
"Fuck man, what you need?"
"Listen bruv…"

Luke went on to explain the situation with his sister and his mum and how Sean had instigated it all and now it was about revenge. Mikaeel agreed with what Luke was saying and even added that he had his own personal problems with Sean. Mikaeel also added that he was rolling in money now so that wouldn't be a problem. Luke acknowledged this.

"When we moving then?"
"Now."
"Now?!"
"Yes bruv, come pick me up. Mitcham station."

Luke hung up. He didn't know for sure if Mikaeel was going to show up, but he would be very surprised if he didn't turn up.

Sure enough, 20 minutes later, Mikaeel rolled up in a blacked-out 4x4 filled with three men in the back and a space for Luke in the front. Mikaeel popped open the door and instructed Luke to get in, handing him a mask as well as a pistol and an Uzi. Luke was taken aback by the level at which Mikaeel seemed to be working. Everything was done cleanly; it was professional – which was going to be necessary if he was going to take down Sean.

The house Sean was supposedly in was only five minutes from the station. Luke instructed Mikaeel to pull over in the street before they got there so he could brief them. Luke turned around to see what he was working with and was met with three menacing individuals, their masks splattered in colour and obscene faces.

"Right, this is the plan."

Luke explained the plan in gross detail. He had been planning this for months and was desperate to get it right. After the brief, he instructed Mikaeel to go meet Bilal at the top of the street and he would drive down and meet them with the others. Mikaeel obliged. He jogged down to meet Bilal as Luke raced past him, sharply turning the corner and zooming down the street. He instinctively braked outside the house and did a handbrake wheelie so the driver's side was facing the house.

As the car ground to a stop, Luke looked up and there he was. Sean Davis. He was just exiting the building, still with the same depressing attire and outdated hair, but he had grown a bit of stubble. Luke acted instantly, not wanting to miss his opportunity. He raised his pistol and fired as many shots as he could toward Sean. This seemed to happen in slow motion as Sean saw the danger and tried to rush back inside. Luke continued to fire shots with no real aim, just in anger. He was firing recklessly to no avail until one made contact with his left leg and another with his hip. The door opened behind him and four men stepped out, firing a spray of bullets toward Luke and his car. Sean crept back as the firing continued. The three men in the back foolishly stepped out and were quickly mowed down by the onslaught.

Luke acted the most efficiently, pulling his window up before pressing on the accelerator and speeding away from the shots. Mikaeel and Bilal sat halfway down the street to watch for police and heard the commotion from a distance. They saw Luke racing towards them, waving his hand frantically at them. They jumped in as Luke pulled over for a second before speeding off again.

"*Fuck!*" Luke screamed in anger.

He slammed harder on the accelerator as he raced away from the scene of the crime. Then his phone rang. It was Sean.

"*You fucking prick!*"

"*Me? You're the one who told Callum to terrorise my family!*"

"*Shut it, you waste of space.*"

"*Lucky I didn't kill you.*"

"*Oh, you'll be lucky if you spend the next 24 hours alive.*"

"*Empty threats.*"

"*I've got a 10k bounty on your head.*"

Luke paused.

"*You hear that, Mikaeel?*"

Luke hung up the phone before throwing it out of the window. He was driving aimlessly but then came up with an idea.

"*Where's your yard, Mikaeel?*"

"*I'm not telling you bruv.*"

Luke nodded toward Bilal who sheepishly reached down to a bag under his seat. He hesitated, but Luke insisted. He pulled out a gun and aimed it at Mikaeel.

"*Tell me, or I'll kill you and find out myself.*"

Mikaeel reluctantly told Luke his address, and Luke stormed over there, sharply turning the corner into his street before pulling up on the pavement outside his house.

"*Get out.*"

Mikaeel sat in his seat as Luke opened the door, the gun still fixed on him. Luke didn't have time for his games and dragged him out of the car, taking the gun off Bilal and placing it in his back. Mikaeel opened his front door, the gun still pressed to his back.

"*Where's the money?*"

"*What? You think I just have it lying around here?*"

"*Where. Is. The. Money.*"

"*No.*"

Luke took a step closer, and instead of using a gun, he drew a knife from his jacket pocket and placed it on Mikaeel's neck. He started to push down, drawing the slightest speck of blood, at which Mikaeel crumbled.

"*Ok fam!*"

"*Where is it?*"

"*In the side door in the top room.*"

Luke signalled for Bilal to go grab it, and within a few minutes, he returned with two briefcases of cash amounting to at least £100,000. Luke smiled as he kept the knife close to Mikaeel's face.

"Look, you've got my money. Now leave."

Luke kept looking at the briefcase while raising his arm and firing three shots into Mikaeel's chest. He stuttered for a moment before giving up and collapsing to the floor. Bilal was in shock.

"Why did you have to shoot him bruv?"

"No witnesses."

Luke closed both suitcases before loading them into the car, and he and Bilal took off.

The day had quietened down from the stress of earlier incidents. Luke and Bilal were still travelling in the car, Luke remaining silent and Bilal confused as to where they were going. They travelled for an hour through Central London before reaching the London Docks. Luke, still eerily silent, pointed for Bilal to get out. The pair moved away from the car to sit right on the edge of the docks as the sun began to set. Luke lit another cigarette and offered one to Bilal, who declined. Bilal was the first to break the silence.

"What are we doing here man?"

"You ever think about the future?"

"Nah, not much."

"I do."

"Stop fucking around man. Why are we here?"

"Stand up."

Luke stood up first with Bilal reluctant to until Luke dragged him up. The sunset was deepening as Luke embraced Bilal in a hug before whispering in his ear.

"It's so good knowing I have someone that'll always have my back."

"Of course, man. We'll be living it up together at the top!"

"There's just one thing."

"What's that?"

Luke broke free from the hug before pushing Bilal down into the water beneath them.

"What… what the fuck bruv?" Bilal spluttered, struggling in the water; he couldn't swim.

"I never told Sean or Callum where I lived."

"Bruv, no! That wasn't me, I swear down!"

"I hope whatever they paid you was worth your life."

Luke flicked his cigarette into the water and walked away. Bilal continued to struggle, screaming out for Luke, but gradually his screams faded into silence.

Luke looked back at the water one last time. It was time for him to disappear.

Part 2

4th *March 2024*

A 22-year-old Ross sat at his desk desperately studying for one of his final exams of the year. He had been at Harvard for the past three years, trying to make it through his degree and reach his dream job. It had been a challenging time. He struggled to make friends, but this was of his own accord; he would rather focus. However, he had grown fond of his roommate, Tyler. He had struggled with some of the work and barely made it through the first year. He didn't let this get him down; he had known it was going to be hard. He just had to keep going with his end goal always in sight. He was currently working on an essay about contract formation and struggling to find precedent to back his argument. He sat frustrated at his screen, smashing the desk a few times in anger. He continued to search until he heard a knock on his door.

"Come in!" Ross called, to no response.

"Tyler!" Still no response.

Ross stormed to the door and swung it open. Tyler stood with a gun to his face and fired instantly. However, instead of bullets, it squirted tequila. Ross stood petrified with his eyes closed until he tasted the liquid that had been sprayed onto his face. Tyler hooted with laughter. Ross slowly opened his eyes and saw Tyler pointing the now obviously fake gun into his mouth and firing multiple times.

"Wheyyyyyyy!"

"What's wrong with you?"

"Just some banter, Ross. Lighten up."

"Well, you've had your fun. I'm gonna go work now."

"Uh-huh-uh, no you're not. We're going to a party!"

"It's 10 am."

"Pool party, bitch!"

Ross stared at Tyler, not believing that this was a Harvard student. Tyler had a knack for acting like an idiot the majority of the time but was actually incredibly smart. He was toward the top of the class rankings and had a stellar record in exams, despite doing next to no work. Tyler continued to pester Ross until he agreed, just to get him off his back. He went back into his room to get ready while Tyler finished off the rest of the tequila gun and let out a happy scream.

Ross smiled as he went to his wardrobe to pick out some things. He loved Tyler, despite his eccentricities. He had no idea where Tyler had sourced this pool party, but seeing he had been working since 5 am, he thought he deserved a day off. He settled on some swimming shorts and a humble T-shirt. He had never been keen on parties or swimming, but he made an exception, especially as Tyler was so excited. Ross had no intention of swimming or staying long; he didn't like his body as it was, and he wasn't keen on everyone seeing it.

As he stepped out of his room, he was met by Tyler standing topless in a bright pink pair of swimming shorts and equally bright neon flip flops. Ross took a moment to look at the monstrosity in front of him and laughed. Tyler wanted to know why he was laughing, but Ross just wanted to get there and get out as quickly as possible. Drunk, Tyler stumbled his way down the stairs supported by Ross. The pair eventually reached the bottom floor and exited through the glass doors. They made their way onto the bus which was just about to depart.

Tyler continued to embarrass himself on the bus journey, with Ross having to control him at times. Tyler was a typical young American man. Originally from Oregon, he played football there as well as for Harvard and he had an impeccable build, which made him appear menacing, but those who knew him knew that he was a massive softy. He pulled out a speaker and decided to blast Katy Perry's Firework and sing along, while Ross struggled to contain his laughter.

They finally arrived at where the pool party was supposed to take place. The driver glared at them as they stepped off, and Ross apologised for Tyler's behaviour. Laughing, they made their way noisily down the street towards the music. When they arrived, instead of going through the front door, Tyler went round to the fence on the side of the property. Thinking he was drunk, Ross tried to direct him to the front door, but Tyler insisted on going through the side.

"This way man!"

"Bro, go through the door."

"We can't."

"Why not?"

"We weren't really invited."

Ross raised his hand to his face and gave a massive sigh.

"What is the plan here exactly?"

"Climb over, run straight into the pool and blend in. Help me up."

Ross reluctantly helped Tyler to get on top of the fence before he assisted Ross up, and the pair made it over seamlessly into some bushes. Tyler whispered to Ross what sounded like gibberish then sprinted toward the pool, screaming, and cannon balled in, creating a huge splash and drawing laughs from all around. There was a massive cheer as he appeared above water with a huge grin

on his face. Ross had seen just about enough. He emerged from
the bushes and went toward the side door to leave.

As he was about to exit, covered in mud, he was halted by a
voice behind him and it wasn't Tyler.

"*Where are you going?*" asked a soft and sweet voice.

Ross turned around to see one of the most beautiful women
he had ever seen. She was in a bikini and had sun-streaked brown
hair, piercing blue eyes and a gleaming smile. Caught up in his
appreciation of the woman in front of him, he forgot to answer
the question; he just stared at her until she snapped her fingers to
bring him back to reality.

"*Yeah, sorry. I was just leaving. Sorry for interrupting.*"

"*No, silly! I saw you guys climb over the fence. It's alright, you
can stay. I assume that's your friend.*"

The girl pointed over to Tyler who was now socialising with
random groups around the pool, pulling off some horrible dance
moves. Ross chuckled before responding.

"*Yeah, that's Tyler.*"

"*Very interesting person. What's your name?*"

"*I'm Ross, and you?*"

"*Jazmine. Do you have an accent?*"

"*Yeah, I'm from the UK.*"

"*Oh wow! Always wanted to go to the UK.*"

Ross continued the conversation, stunned that a girl of this
level was even talking to him. They chatted until Tyler shouted
something to Ross, making sexual gestures with his hands, making
both of them laugh. Ross told Jazmine that he'd better go save
Tyler before he was sick or embarrassed himself even more.
Jazmine agreed but didn't let Ross leave without giving him her
number. Ross willingly took it down before hugging her goodbye
and walking over to Tyler.

"*Ross! Rossathan, Rossgod, Rosspussyman?*"

"Let's go, Tyler."

Ross laughed as he helped Tyler out of the pool and managed him successfully until his stomach gave in and he vomited in the bushes where they had first hidden. Ross placed his hand on Tyler's back, encouraging him to get it all out, while looking over at Jazmine and apologising. Tyler claimed he had finished but doubled over and threw up again. As he finished up, he looked deflated and defeated but not for long.

The speakers kicked in, blasting out Glass Animals' Heat Waves. Tyler seemed to forget about his apparent weakness and jumped back into the mosh pit that had started near the pool. Ross tried to stop him, but he was a livewire and he looked as though he was enjoying himself, so Ross let him be. Ross's phone rang and dispayed an unknown number. He reluctantly picked up.

"Hey, stranger."

Ross recognized the voice instantly and his reluctance turned to excitement as he looked up to see Jazmine smiling and waving to him.

"Hey, sorry about him."

"It's ok… Hey, it's almost midday. Do you wanna walk and get some food?"

"Sure."

Ross hung up and walked over to Jazmine, instructing a few people to look after Tyler while he was gone, knowing he couldn't control himself. Jazmine and Ross exited the party through the front door this time, Jaz throwing on a baggy hoodie to cover her bikini.

"Is this your house?" Ross enquired.

"Yeah, I don't really like mentioning it; it's more my parents'."

"Still, it's really nice."

"Yeah, well my mum is a surgeon, and my dad is a lawyer, so a lot to live up to."

"Yeah, I can imagine."

"What about your parents?"

Ross paused.

"Sorry, I didn't mean to get too personal."

"Nah, it's ok, my mum was a community nurse and I never really knew my dad; he died early."

"Oh, I'm sorry. Do you wanna talk about it?"

As they continued down the street, Ross went into more detail about his life and background, and Jazmine listened intently. He had never really had an outlet to express his emotions so it was a relief to have someone finally listen. He gave her details about his brother and his psychiatric disorder. He felt bad for talking so much about himself, but Jazmine reassured him it was ok; then he asked her about herself. Jazmine had come from an affluent but strict background; her mum and dad expected a lot from her, and this made her feel very pressured and anxious. The two found comfort in each other as they reached the closest McDonald's.

Despite the seriousness of the conversation on the journey, the two managed to joke around as they entered McDonald's, laughing and giggling at random things which normally wouldn't be funny. Ross paid for both their meals, although it was only McDonald's. His mum had taught him to always treat a woman like a queen, always appreciate her and never apologise for being a nice guy, although she warned him that many girls in his generation wouldn't appreciate or understand this. She taught him to always love with his whole heart, even if it might end in pain. Ross wasn't in love; he had only met this girl once, but the principle of treating a woman like a queen still held.

When they returned to the party, Jazmine stopped Ross as they were about to go in.

"Do you wanna go to a movie instead? It's literally just round the corner."

Ross desperately wanted to go but knew he couldn't leave Tyler on his own. Jazmine desperately wanted to see a new film just out, so he told her he would check on Tyler as Jazmine had reassured him that her parents were home and would look after him. Ross rushed in, asking around for Tyler and finding him lounging on a deck chair. Tyler held up a finger, shades covering his eyes.

"Go secure that bag, king."

Ross laughed as he spudded Tyler and walked out. Jazmine had changed into shorts and a simple shirt. Her change of clothes made Ross very self-conscious about what he was wearing; turning up to the cinema in swimming shorts was not the best fashion statement. He asked Jazmine if he could quickly go home and change, but she chuckled before saying it didn't matter, it was a drive-in theatre. Ross was confused as Jazmine lead him to the garage revealing a Tesla.

"Wow!" Ross exclaimed.

"It's not mine, but my mum said I could take it out once a month – no time like now."

Ross smiled as he took the passenger seat. This girl was full of surprises. She started the car and exited flawlessly. Ross posed another question to Jazmine.

"Jazmine…"

"Call me Jaz – you aren't my auntie," Jaz joked.

"Sorry, Jaz. Aren't drive-in cinemas only open at night?"

"Right again, Mr Intelligent."

"Shut up," Ross joked as he cracked another smile. *"Where are we going then?"*

"You'll see."

Jaz drove on, blasting her music through the speakers and singing along. Ross took a second to look at her. As she caught him staring, she smiled even more and told him to put a song on. The pressure was on. Ross prided himself on his musical taste, but most of his listening was UK music. He searched for a few minutes while Jaz became curious about what he was going to pick. Eventually, he found one of his favourite songs by an American artist and put it on. As soon Jaz heard the intro, she squealed with excitement and she gripped his hand.

"I love Dominic Fike!"

They listened to the long intro of King of Everything and sang together as the song kicked in. It was a perfect moment.

They took turns to pick songs and impress each other with their musical taste, some of which was very similar. Eventually, Jaz pulled the car to a stop at the foot of a large hill. With no idea of what they were going to do, Ross jumped out the car and followed Jaz as she led him up the hill. He couldn't believe where he was and who he was with. He let his thoughts wander for a moment until Jaz yelled down to him telling him how slow he was. He instantly accepted the challenge and caught up to her, the grabbed her by the waist. They laughed and giggled as Jaz broke away to show Ross what they had come to see.

She led him to a small bench on the top of the hill with a small engraving on it. Seated on the bench, they gazed out across the city beneath them.

"It's so peaceful up here," she started. *"You can take a break from everything, all the stress in the world, all the busyness of everyday life. You can come here and just relax."*

"Is that why you brought me here?"

"You really are an idiot, aren't you?"

"What?" Ross responded sarcastically before play fighting with her.

After a couple of minutes, they paused, face to face. Ross was afraid. He hadn't even had his first kiss yet, and he had no idea how he'd even made it to this situation. He stared at her blankly as she closed her eyes and leaned toward him. Ross panicked momentarily before doing the same. They kissed as the sun set and decided to abandon the film to just talk.

When Ross checked his watch, he saw it was almost 8 pm. He told Jaz he had to get back to Tyler; he was a child and couldn't be left on his own for long. Jaz agreed, realising she had abandoned her own party. They made their way down the hill as the night conquered the skyline. They climbed back in the Tesla and exchanged music again, more mellow tones this time as they made their way back.

Jaz and Ross returned to a much quieter house; the music had stopped and the house seemed empty. Ross began to panic. He rushed to the front door, Jaz just behind him. He knocked on the door, which Jaz's dad answered.

"Hello, young man. I see you're the one who abducted my daughter for the day!"

"Sorry, sir."

"Only joking mate. Hope you had a good time. I assume he is yours, too."

Jaz's dad pointed over at Tyler who sat in the living room almost passed out, muttering something, with his head resting on his shoulder. Red with embarrassment, Ross rushed over to Tyler to wake him up.

"Rosssssssssss."

"Yeah, it's me. Come on, let's go."

"Okayyyyyyyyy!"

Ross helped Tyler to his feet and to the door, apologising to Jaz's dad for his behaviour. He laughed off Ross's apology, and Ross thanked him for his hospitality. He went outside where Jaz was standing, still giggling to herself. Tyler managed to break free from Ross's support and stumbled over to Jaz.

"You see this man over here?" he spluttered, and Ross rolled his eyes. *"Marry him!"*

"Right, that's enough."

Ross hauled Tyler away before hugging Jaz goodbye.

"I'll see you soon, yeah?"

"Yeah, for sure, just text me."

"Marry him!" Tyler yelled out again.

The pair laughed at him as Ross lead him away before he caused any more damage. They were halfway down the street before Tyler spoke again.

"Soooooooo."

"Shut up man." Ross chuckled.

"What happened? Tell me everything!"

"No, a gentleman never tells."

"A gentleman! Ross Susans, you are the furthest thing from a gentleman."

"Ok, maybe I got a kiss."

Tyler leapt with excitement before pulling Ross in for a hug and whooping with joy.

"Yes, Ross Susans. Fucking finally!"

"Shut up man, it's no big deal."

"If you want me to shut up, I guess I won't tell you what I got up to."

Ross was intrigued as Tyler grinned broadly

"Go on then!"

"Well…"

"Yes!"

"I got with someone."

"Who? What's her name?"

"No, Ross, his name."

Ross's jaw fell to the ground. He had always wondered whether Tyler was gay, but he had only seen him get with girls so had quickly put that suspicion to rest, too scared to ask him.

"His? You're gay?"

"Not gay, I'm bi. I'm surprised you haven't worked it out by now."

Ross pulled Tyler in and gave him a hug, catching him by surprise. Ross strongly believed that it didn't matter who you were in any sense, including sexuality, race or even what your favourite colour was. He respected everyone and was incredibly proud of Tyler for telling him.

"Good for you man! I'm proud of you."

"Really?"

"Of course, man. I still love you the same."

Tyler broke into tears and gave Ross another hug. He had been ostracised by most people in his life when talking about his sexuality, most notably his parents who were very religious and traditional. The pair got on the bus to return to their accommodation, both with smiles on their faces.

The dusty, dirty seats gave off a repulsive smell as the bus trickled along the half-made road to its destination. Luke sat closely guarding a bag he had placed on the seat next to him. He was travelling through New Mexico on his way to meet some new recruits. In four years, Luke had escaped from London to Mexico unharmed after his altercations with the SD. He had started with a small business pushing and moving product. It was easier than in London due to more relaxed legislation regarding drugs. He became known around Mexico as *"El Loco"* due to the various methods he used. He was now an established drug kingpin, fighting off other Mexican cartels that tried to challenge him. He was ruthless and left no witnesses when executing his work.

He stared out of the poor excuse of a window, his black shades masking the true colour of the landscape. He was dripped out in al-black attire, strange for a place so blazing hot, especially at this time of year. When the bus reached the outskirts of the city,

Luke stepped out, throwing an uncounted number of pesos at the driver to keep him quiet. People were always after Luke, both from London and now locally; he had to stay as hidden as possible.

Throwing his bag over his shoulder, he soldiered on through the light wind and dust. He walked for around a mile till he arrived at his destination. He wrapped his bandana around his mouth and burst into the abandoned warehouse without warning. Luke had a tough recruitment process. He put forward only people he could trust and killed those who didn't qualify. He saw four individuals being forced to kneel down with bags covering their heads. Luke instructed his current workmen to take off the bags and introduced himself to the men.

"Hola las idiotas! Just kidding. I'm going to speak English. Quien no puede hablar Ingles?"

One individual raised his hand sheepishly. Luke laughed before opening his bag and going over to the man. He was skinny, with bags under his eyes, and clearly left with no option but to live this life. Luke threw the bag down in front of the man and asked him his name. As the man was about to answer, Luke drew a pistol from his bag and shot him in the head.

"No messing around!"

The other individuals looked on in horror at how quickly Luke had made his decision. Luke went over to one of the men holding the other three candidates and whispered in his ear.

"Unfortunately, I've been informed one of you is a snake. Now, I could stand here and meticulously try and work this out. But I'm not patient enough for that."

Luke signalled to his worker who swiftly knocked all three of them dead on the floor. Luke was annoyed he had wasted a trip, but in the business he was in, he had to be careful. He could have no friends, as he had learned back in London.

"Come."

Despite being somewhat reckless, Luke had a strategic mind. He'd had a feeling that this little meeting wouldn't lead to much, so he'd made sure it was held near one of his opposition's main drug operations disguised as a clothing factory. Luke led his four men outside, all wearing masks and not saying much. Luke kept his staff quiet and efficient, and they listened respectfully out of fear of death. Even being on his side was no guarantee of safety; one mistake and you could be wiped out.

The five men made their way to a Mercedes G Wagon parked outside, all blacked out. Luke sat in the passenger seat as one of the men drove. The short journey was completed in silence as Luke slipped on his mask and attached his pistol to his waist. He decided to lead with the Uzi, which he prepped as the car pulled up outside. It was lunchtime, so many of the factory workers were exiting the building. This didn't faze Luke as he stepped out firing multiple shots into the air, dispersing the crowd. He led his small army smashing through the doors, setting off the alarm and alerting those in the back office, the ones that really ran the operation.

Factory workers panicked as Luke's men shot random workers dead to incite a response. Eventually, the back-office men mobilised and rushed out of the office, all armed. The difference between the two sides was the training. Luke not only made his recruitment exclusive, but he trained up his men to have the advantage in these sorts of situations. This worked in their favour as they quickly and efficiently took out the opposition, who were clueless in their approach.

After dispatching those men, Luke and his posse pushed on, leaving no man with a gun alive. Luke smashed down the door to the office to reveal a cowardly-looking individual sitting at his desk.

"*Carlos! Como estas?*"

"Vete a la mierda, perra."

"No way to talk to your new business partner, surely!"

"Fuck you."

"Look at that, he speaks English!"

Luke kept his gun aimed at Carlos as he picked up a bin off the floor, emptied it and passed it to one of his workmen, instructing him to go fill it with water.

"Where's your product?"

"Fuck you."

"Someone clearly didn't take many English lessons."

His man promptly returned with the bin filled with water and handed it to Luke. Luke instructed his men to grab Carlos and pin him down to the chair, and Luke approached with the bin full of water.

"See normally, I would just put a bullet in your head and find it myself. But that's no fun."

Luke held the bucket behind Carlos's head and instructed his workmen to lift him and dunk his head into the water. After 30 seconds, Luke indicated to lift him out.

"It's in the machines!" Carlos gasped.

"Good boy, drown him."

"What? But –"

Luke handed the water to one of the men and made his way downstairs to the machines. The place had been cleared out, and Luke pulled down his mask and slipped on a glove before carefully opening up one of the machines. Sure enough, the machine wasn't functional at all; it was just filled with Grade A cocaine. Luke took a pinch and tasted it just to check. He raised a thumbs up to the office as they finished drowning Carlos, and all the men walked out, still wearing their masks.

"There's too much here to move. We'll take this warehouse for ourselves," Luke stated.

The men nodded in unison and instantly got to work checking the building for any remaining workers and rounding them up in front of Luke, who had made his way up to the balcony ready to speak, one of his men standing next to him as a translator.

"Listen up. You work for me now. Anything Carlos had you doing, you keep doing but for me. If any of you mess me around or try and snake me, I will bury you, and then your family. Understood?"

The workers, clearly alarmed, all agreed and quickly got to work. Luke left the balcony with his translator and rounded up his men, giving them instructions to look after the warehouse. If there were any issues, he should be called; he had a meeting to attend.

Luke casually exited the warehouse, his mask now back on, and jumped into the car. He quickly drove off and after an hour reached the town of Nogales, situated right on the border between the US and Mexico. Luke had built up his reputation in Mexico, but his long-term plan always involved the United States. It was perfect for his business and required less of the dirty side he had to manage here in Mexico. He stopped at a small gas station, took a three-piece suit from the boot and purchased a razor from the shop. In the grimy gas station toilets, he changed into the suit and trimmed his stubble to look presentable. This meeting was important.

He was meeting with Raquel Marquez, the queenpin in the Mexican drug game. Raquel and Luke had a mutual understanding: they would not target each other to avoid all-out war, but now he had the chance to turn it into a partnership. Raquel was perhaps as unpredictable as Luke. No one knew her full story for sure. What was common knowledge was that she had killed her husband, Antonio Marquez, to get control of his drug business. Like Luke, she had a long rap sheet and was not afraid to extend it. This was the link into the US Luke had been chasing for years, ever since he'd arrived in Mexico, and now Raquel had an opportunity for him. The struggle Luke always had was getting across the border. Sean was still after him, so he had to change his identity and very few people knew his real name or where he came from. Crossing the border with fake identification risked being caught by police or, even worse, one of Sean's men whom he had situated around the world.

Freshly kitted out, Luke made his way back to his car, putting his shades back on and looking more like a man who would drive the car he was driving. Five minutes later, he pulled up outside a stunning piece of modern architecture. Costing somewhere between three and four million dollars, the impressive structure was lined with glass decorated with extravagant white streaks masking the stylish interior. Luke stepped out of his car, fastening his suit button and checking himself for blood, before approaching the two security guards at the gate. They checked him for any threat before scanning him and letting him through the gate. He walked up the driveway and was about to knock on the door when it opened for him, revealing Raquel dressed in equally smooth attire, a woman of pure class.

"*Come in,*" she insisted.

"*That's why I'm here,*" Luke said sarcastically. He had not lost that side of him.

Raquel led Luke through the house to the living room, elegantly picked up her glass of wine, and took a seat on her perfect sofa, indicating for Luke to do the same.

"*Now Luke –*"

"*I'll start.*" Raquel was a bit taken aback but let him continue.

"*Combined, we are worth about 10 million. Now the market in Mexico is good, but there's too much risk. Let me expand into America, and we'll earn double, together.*"

Raquel replaced her wine on the table and stared up at Luke.

"*You know I killed my husband.*"

"*Yes, I'm aware.*"

"*He was a pig, an imbecile. No room for new ideas or expanding the business. He settled for mediocre. I am not mediocre.*"

"*I know; that's why I want to expand here.*"

"*I slit his throat.*"

"*Yeah, good for you. What about the deal?*"

"*You are rash, Luke. I don't like rash.*"

"*I'm not rash, I'm efficient.*"

"*60 recorded deaths are linked to you. That's just recorded.*"

"*Efficient.*"

"*Reckless.*"

Raquel drew a pistol from her dress, placing it down on the glass table in front of her and pointing it toward Luke.

"*I don't do partnerships, you see.*"

"*Neither do I. We don't have to be partners. We just have things in common, like money.*"

"*I need proof you won't betray me.*"

"*Proof?*"

Raquel leaned in closer toward Luke as if to kiss him. Luke closed his eyes, expecting a kiss. Instead, Raquel gripped him by the throat, forcing his eyes open.

"*Typical man. Women aren't just for sexual use, you imbecile.*"

"*Let go.*"

Raquel relaxed her grip on Luke before straightening her dress and relaxing back down onto her sofa.

"*I can get you into America, into LA.*"

"*LA?*"

"*I have people elsewhere; my main man in LA got caught, and I need a replacement.*"

"*I'll take it, but I don't work for you.*"

Raquel stared at Luke angrily.

"*What part of this are you not getting? Everyone works for me.*"

"Not me."

The two had a brief staredown, the gun still on the table, tempting both. Luke broke the silence.

"I'll run LA, as your equal."

"Ok Luke, you'll have LA as my equal. You'll have lots to move, and you'll have a team ready there."

"I use my team."

"You're really making this difficult, aren't you?"

"I'm a businessman."

"Ok, you take your team. If I don't see results in the first month, I'll shoot them all myself and finish with you by slitting your throat."

"I'm the same level as your husband then?"

"Get out."

Two men appeared behind Luke, ready to escort him out. He slowly got up, fastening his suit jacket again before extending a hand to Raquel. She turned her head away as the men ushered Luke away. They quickly moved Luke out of the building and back to his car, watching intently as he drove away. He pulled up his phone and called Alejandro, the leader of his little group and Luke's right-hand man. He was one of the few people who knew Luke and who he was and where he came from. Luke trusted Alejandro. He never involved him in the shooting business; he was a useful accountant and money manager. Luke had employed him as soon as he'd arrived in Mexico as he already knew English and was recently graduated with no work. Alejandro had helped Luke set up his empire and had never betrayed him in the four years he had been in Mexico.

"Alejandro!"

"Yes, Luke, what's up?"

"Guess who's going to America bruv."

"Fuck yes!"

Alejandro whooped in excitement. He had been trying for years to enter America, to no avail. The pair discussed the plan and their future until Luke was approaching his home, located in Hermosillo. A humbler home than Raquel's but comfortable enough to live in and humble enough that no one would ask questions. Luke pulled up outside his house and jumped out, to be greeted by Alejandro sitting at his gate.

"Mr Americano!"

"Shut up, you idiot." Laughing, Luke embraced Alejandro.

He had never been able to trust anyone fully, but Alejandro he trusted the most. He had never given him reason to doubt him and had been loyal since the start. The two walked into Luke's house, and he opened up a fresh bottle of whiskey he had been saving for this occasion. He slid a glass across to Alejandro.

"You want to know how much you made this month?"

"No."

"What, why?"

"I wanna know how much we made."

Luke and Alejandro smiled and looked over the work of the past month. It had been a successful month for Luke and his team, accumulating over $200,000 from their various activities. The two looked over the plan going forward and devised a system they would use when they got to the US. It was a lot harder there, so they had to be careful. After spending a few hours devising their game plan in great detail, the two kicked back and watched some tv, a moment of peace in a world of chaos. After their short break, Luke started to get things ready. He assumed he was going as soon as possible so he had already started clearing out his house, disposing of any evidence. Alejandro assisted him and within two hours, the work was done.

"That's it, Alejandro. We're going to America."

28th September 2024

"This way Jaz!" Ross called across the frosty lawn. The pair had decided to move in together for their final year at Harvard, the crunch year. The two had been dating for six months, having got together in April after their first encounter back in March. Ross did feel bad for leaving Tyler, but he had found a place with his football friends and the two vowed to stay in contact despite not sharing a room.

Ross had become infatuated with Jazmine. The last six months had been the most interesting, exciting and amazing time of his life. He had even managed to introduce Jazmine to his mum via Facetime, and, of course, she overwhelmingly approved. Today, the couple were moving into their new flat, perfectly situated next to the hill with the bench where they'd shared their first kiss. Ross had done the majority of the moving; he had been building up his strength by going to the gym and eating properly, sculpting himself into a man he could be proud of.

Ross carried a table into their new flat, which lay bare but for a West Ham poster he had stuck up before anything else. They had agreed to just get the basic stuff in first and sort out the mess later. At the end of the long day, the couple cuddled up on their sofa in front of the tv, currently propped up against the wall.

"I love you."

"I love you too."

They exchanged a kiss before Jaz got up and went to get ready. Ross was confused for a second, thinking he had missed an important date again, until he remembered that she was going out to celebrate her friend's birthday. He didn't mind much; he had some work to get done and also fancied a quiet night on his own. As Jaz unpacked some clothes from the suitcase on the floor, Ross called out to her.

"Do you want me to pick you up?" He had also recently passed his driving test.

"Nah it's ok, Lily's friend is going to give me a lift home."

"Alright, no worries."

Ross paid no real attention to Jaz going out. He trusted her and was confident their bond was unbreakable. He still planned to pick her up and surprise her by taking her to get some food after the party. She was always hungry after a night out. Ross had planned this with one of her friends, Samantha.

Jaz took the better part of an hour to get ready while Ross browsed Netflix and sorted some stuff out around the flat. Eventually, Jaz's noisy friends turned up, and they all cheered as she emerged in a stunning dress. Ross waved to the group as they roared off, with Samantha giving him a wink regarding the plan they had hatched.

Ross retreated into the flat, sat on the sofa and opened his laptop to get on with some work. Seconds turned into hours as he tried to prepare an argument for the next day's mock trial, a very important one not just for his degree but for his record. He hadn't lost one since arriving at Harvard. Ross gradually dozed off until his phone rang at 2 am. Blinking, he saw it was Samantha ringing him. Realising he was late, he jumped off the sofa and rushed to the car, assuring Samantha he would be there in five minutes.

He managed to make his way over in three and pulled up outside the club the girls had been to. Samantha rushed over to him with two of her other friends, but there was no sign of Jaz.

"Where's Jaz?"

"We can't find her."

Ross jumped out of the car and went to the club to look for Jaz. As he tried to gain entry, he was stopped by the bouncers demanding his ID. He realised that in his rush he had left his wallet with his ID at home, so he gave the bouncers a description and asked them to look for her. The bouncers checked inside but told Ross that she had been seen leaving. Ross panicked and began searching the area. At the end of an alley round the side of the club, he made out two figures. As he drew closer, he recognized the dress Jaz had been wearing.

"*Jaz!*" he shouted.

The two figures stopped interacting, and a male voice responded.

"*Who you?*"

Ross' heart sank.

"*Jaz?*" he asked more gently.

"*What are you doing here Ross?*" Jaz replied as her face came into the light.

Her hair was messed up, her makeup smudged and her bra straps showing. Tears pricked Ross's eyes as the man stepped into the light. Ross paid no attention to the guy; his eyes were fixed on Jaz who couldn't look him in the eyes. Ross's heart was shattered; he couldn't believe what he was seeing. He looked at her for a few more seconds, then turned away without saying another word and stormed back to his car. Jaz called out to him, but he didn't look back. When he returned to his car, he found the three girls sitting inside.

"*Get out.*"

"*Ross, what happened?*" Samantha attempted.

"*Get out.*"

Without further prompting, the girls climbed out and Ross shot off. With tears streaming down his face, he stepped down harder on the accelerator and zoomed past his house, parking instead at the bottom of the hill. He climbed to the top and sat on the bench in silence for a while. He couldn't process his emotions, a bundle of anger, sadness, frustration and hate toward this girl. He didn't understand; he'd done everything his mum had told him to do, but he recalled her warning about girls in this generation.

Ross smacked the bench beneath him violently and burst into tears again. He'd never understood what people meant by heartbreak, always thinking that they were exaggerating, but now what he felt was more painful than anything he had ever experienced.

He put his AirPods in as music was his escape from the world; it helped him describe his emotions in a way he had never been able to before, and he needed it now more than ever. He went onto Spotify and pulled up his sad playlist; he had a playlist for every emotion but rarely used this one. He hit shuffle and The Night We Met by Lord Huron blared out. He hadn't realised his volume was on full, but he decided to keep it there, so he didn't hear the rustling behind him as someone approached. It was Jaz.

She put her hand on Ross's shoulder which made him leap off the bench and pause his music. They stared at each other with tears in their eyes. Jaz broke the silence.

"Ross –"

"Don't."

"Bu —"

"I loved you..."

Ross's voice broke every time he attempted to speak. Jaz continued to speak, but Ross paid no attention. He pressed play on his music as there was nothing she could say which would diminish his pain. Jaz noticed he wasn't listening and took a step toward him, but he did the opposite, distancing himself from her again. He didn't know for certain how to deal with this pain, but he knew that listening to her excuses wouldn't help.

Ross contemplated just walking away but noticed Jaz had stopped talking and was sitting on the bench, her head in her hands. He took his AirPods out and heard her sobbing. Ross sat next to her, placing his arm around her shoulders. She looked up with a smile and a sense of relief. Ross was quick to dismiss this; he shook his head, indicating that he was not accepting what had happened. He just couldn't see her cry like that, despite what she had done to him. He had to make sure she was ok. The two sat for an hour in near silence, Ross with his arm still wrapped around her. He broke the silence this time.

"*I have to go.*"

"*I'll come with you!*" Jaz whispered hopelessly.

"*Jaz. We're done.*"

Ross spoke softly, without aggression. There was no need for hostility or a messy breakup. Ross had his own personal goals to pursue, and he couldn't be held down by what had happened. He got up and looked Jaz in the eye one more time before walking down to the hill to where he had left his car parked askew. He drove the short journey back to their flat, but once inside, he collapsed on the sofa, his hands on his head. He let out a scream, to no response, almost as if the universe was echoing the fact that he was now alone. He looked at the time and panicked when he realised he had his mock trial in less than three hours and still had tons to prepare. He set to work immediately, seemingly forgetting about the emotional turmoil he had just been through. Ross always wanted to work; he had a passion for throwing himself into work, especially when he was feeling down. It was a distraction, an outlet.

He stared blankly at his laptop, trying to make sense of the mess he had composed the previous night. He tried to add some direction to his argument, but at every attempt, he was met with writer's block. After a while, he angrily slammed his laptop shut and curled up into a little ball on the sofa.

Luke and Alejandro sat silently in the back of a taxi making their way to Raquel's house. Today was the day the pair would make the move to America after years of slogging it out in Mexico. Now, they finally had a chance to make the transition they had been so desperate for. They had no clear idea what the plan was; they had just been given a time to meet and told to come with nothing but themselves. The rest of Luke's team had already made the journey across the border in several staggered groups to avoid suspicion, but Luke insisted on travelling with Alejandro to make sure his right-hand man got across safely.

The taxi had been sent by Raquel and had picked them up from Luke's house sharply at 9 am. The driver deposited them at the entrance to her enormous property, and they went through the same security precautions Luke had been through the first time he had visited.

They were met by Raquel in another silky dress, with a collection of items laid out in front of her, including two passports, a change of clothes, a razor and, of course, two pistols. Luke surveyed the equipment in front of him. It looked so simple he questioned his need for Raquel in the whole operation. He paid particular attention to the razor.

"Why this?"

"You're both shaving your heads."

"What?" Alejandro exclaimed.

"You wanted my help, you do this."

Reluctantly, Luke took the razor first and was marshalled by one of the guards to the bathroom. He raised the razor to his head and began to trim his luxuriant locks which he had cultivated during his time in Mexico. The job completed, he examined himself in the mirror. He looked like a younger version of himself. The guard bust through the door and instructed him to go back to the table. Raquel didn't take any chances, especially in her own house. Luke returned to snickers from Alejandro at his new look. Luke smacked him round the head before handing him the razor and sending him off with the guard. He turned to Raquel.

"What's all this, then?"

"The razor, to change your look. The passports, new identities and the guns… well they should be pretty self-explanatory."

"Easy enough."

Luke expected a little more but sensed there was part of the plan Raquel was not telling him. Regardless, he didn't have an option at this point. Raquel was his best chance of getting into America, and he was far too invested now to back out.

Alejandro returned a few moments later with an equally absurd look at which Luke chuckled. The pair always had a touch of humour wherever they went, even in a situation as serious as this. Raquel invited the two to take a seat at the table and began to explain the plan. She left out no detail and seemed to have covered every possible outcome. She asked the pair whether they had any questions, but the plan seemed simple enough. In a nutshell, she would cause a distraction by recruiting many hopefuls like Luke and Alejandro to rush the part of the border they were trying to get through; the same plan had worked for Luke's team a few weeks earlier. In the chaos, Luke and Alejandro should easily be allowed access sitting in the back of a car driven by one of Raquel's guards. They agreed to the plan and began to get ready. It was all happening.

The wheels were soon in motion. They were escorted to the exit by one of the guards, and Luke went to shake Raquel's hand.

"Shake my hand when you bring me results."

Luke drew back his hand, careful not to respond in anger as he so often did in these kinds of situations. He bit his lip and nodded to her before leaving the house with Alejandro. One of the guards remained in position at the entrance to the house, and one followed them down to their car. The guard hopped in the front, instructing the two to get in the back.

The three set off down the broken road to the border. They had only one shot at this, so it had to count. Luke focused himself and could sense Alejandro was nervous, mostly from the pool of sweat that had collected on his seat. He pulled him closer to him and promised him this was it; he was finally getting out.

Alejandro had not had the easiest of upbringings, which was one of the reasons Luke had taken such a shine to him. Growing up in a shanty town, he had been abandoned by his mother at an early age and had to escape from his abusive father at the age of 15. He managed to work his way to university but could not afford to continue past the year when Luke had picked up on his talent for numbers and finance and hired him instantly. Luke gave Alejandro an opportunity in a life that seemed bleak, and he was forever in his debt.

Near the border, they were told to get ready. The process was simple enough. The driver would say he was taking two tourists home while slipping the guard some extra money not to raise the alarm. The other illegal immigrants would rush that part of the border, which would divert the guards' attention away from Luke and Alejandro, allowing them access without further questioning. Easy in theory, it could prove difficult in practice.

As they approached the border, the guard called the leader of the group to get into position. They only had one chance at this, with a chance of prison time or even death if they didn't get it right.

The car pulled into border control; it was deserted. A guard approached the window and knocked on the glass. The driver pulled the window down and exchanged a few words in Spanish that Luke couldn't quite make out. After their brief conversation, Luke and Alejandro passed their fake passports forward for the guard to check. He briefly inspected them before moving to the back window to see their faces.

"*Sal, por favor.*"

"*Que?*"

Without hesitation, the guard pulled the door open, dragged Alejandro out and forced him to the floor, pinning him down with his knee with his hands behind his back.

"*Bro, what the fuck!*" Luke yelled.

"*Stay!*" the guard instructed Luke before closing the door.

Luke rushed over to Alejandro's side of the car to see what was happening. The guard said something else in Spanish to the driver before he sped off through the border, leaving Alejandro behind.

"*Turn the fuck around!*"

"*No.*"

"*Where the fuck is the mob?*"

"*Raquel will call you.*"

"*You fucking prick.*"

Luke reached forward and grabbed the shirt of the driver, causing the car to swerve until he pulled over. Luke knocked him out with his pistol as the car came to a stop and dragged him out the car before instantly calling Raquel.

"*Yo, what the fuck? We had a deal.*"

"*We still do have a deal.*"

"*I said, my team!*"

"*And you will have your team. Just not Alejandro.*"

"*Let him through.*"

"*Think of it as an exchange. You'll get him back if you deliver my results.*"

"*I told you, I don't work for you.*"

"*See, here is the issue, Luke. You do. And if you don't, I'll kill your little pet project.*" "*What happened to the fucking immigrant rush?*"

"*You really are naïve.*"

"*Fucking bitch.*"

"*And volatile! I already control all of border control. Anything I want to get through can get through.*"

Luke smashed the dashboard of the car as he thought about spinning around to rescue Alejandro.

"*Give me him, now.*"

"*Why do you care so much about this kid? There's a million like him.*"

"*You fucking bitch, I'm gonna go get him.*"

"*By the time you get to him, he'll be dead. And their next instructions will be to shoot you.*"

"*Fuck sake!*" Luke screamed.

"*Go do my work, we won't have an issue.*"

"*You'll regret this.*"

Luke slammed down the phone and threw a couple of punches at the steering wheel in front of him. He had half a mind to turn around and kill Raquel, but he knew he had been outsmarted, so much so that it had brought out the old side of him, the violent and reckless side. Luke put his anger to the side for a moment as he sorted out the car and continued his journey. Welcome to America, Luke Moffat.

Ross rushed up the stairs toward the entrance of Harvard Law, already late for his mock trial. The events of the previous 24 hours were still fresh in his mind as he sprinted through the hallway, drawing stares from other students. He turned a corner sharply, bumping into one of his professors, Dr Mansell.

"*Watch it!*"

"*Sorry Miss, I'm late.*"

"*Don't be late then!*"

Ross smiled for the first time in hours as he continued to the lecture hall where the trial was taking place. Most of the lecturers hated him as he was seen as lazy or not as hardworking as some of the other Harvard students. Ross paid no attention to this narrative; he had experienced this since school. Dr Mansell was an exception; she always took time to converse with Ross, even after lectures, and the pair had a good relationship.

When Ross burst through the doors of the lecture theatre, the trial had already started. He was aware that every pair of eyes was fixed on him. He tried to play it off, walking through the waves of students up to the top of the lecture theatre.

"Good you could join us, Mr Susans! I'll be sure to note that down."

"Sorry, sir," Ross replied meekly.

Luckily, the trial before his had overrun so he had made it in time for his turn. He opened his notes and his laptop simultaneously, trying to stuff in as much detail about the pending case as he could. The time came for him to take part in the mock trial. It was a domestic abuse case. Fictional characters Clifford Young and Maria Lemos had been in a loveless marriage for the last 20 years and this had resulted in many arguments. On one occasion, Clifford claimed, Maria had hit him over the head with a vase and verbally assaulted him after an argument about the time he arrived home from work. Ross had been assigned to Clifford's side, not knowing who his opposition would be as the original opposition had dropped out of Harvard a week before the mock trial.

He made his way down the stairs from the top of the lecture theatre, his notes clutched firmly against his chest. As he reached the front of the room, he approached the table carelessly, spilling his books over the table and drawing a stare of disdain from the lecturer playing judge. He sat down, cleared his throat and held up his hand in apology. He scanned the room for his opponent but couldn't see anyone moving to the front. For a moment he thought he would automatically be given the victory, but then a girl burst through the closed doors to Ross's left. He was shocked to see a short blonde with glasses staring at him. He knew her. Chloe Mitchener stood before him, a deep enemy from school.

She smirked at him before walking through the theatre, apologising for being late by putting a hand up toward the lecturer. The majority of the lecturers didn't like Ross, but they all had a burning hatred for Chloe. She was smart, yes, but she always thought she was the most intelligent person in the room, even smarter than her lecturers. The judge decided not to penalise Chloe as Ross had also been late. She stepped up to the table, looked Ross up and down and took her seat.

The judge began the trial by welcoming opening statements, starting with the defendant, Maria Lemos. Chloe stood up and with gleaming confidence took the short walk to centre stage before turning to the jury.

"Ladies and gentlemen of the esteemed jury. This case is straight forward. No matter what the prosecution tries to argue, there is no clear evidence linking my client to any of the crimes of which she is accused. Maria has no clear history of violence. Multiple people she's met and worked with say she is the furthest thing from a violent person, and as this trial goes on, we will prove that fully. Thank you, your honour."

Chloe spun round and strode back to her seat, still staring at Ross. She had entered the fray with clarity and speed. Ross was a bit dazed, confused by her constant gaze as well as her solid performance. It wasn't until the judge's second call that Ross snapped into focus and nervously hopped out of his seat to face the jury. Time slowed and his heart pounded in his chest as he examined the eyes focused on him. He took a deep breath before he spoke.

> *"Ladies and gentlemen of the jury. Clifford has been suffering in an abusive relationship for years, being manipulated, gas lighted and forced to do things he did want to do. He has been brave enough to speak out about his experiences to date, climaxing in a physical attack for which, I assure you, there is plenty of evidence. This trial will consider many instances of abuse, and I want to emphasise the strength of this man to speak out about such trauma. Thank you, your honour."*

Ross swivelled round, staring at Chloe as he marched back to his seat. The two hadn't communicated verbally, but the tension was noticeable to all. They were both now more motivated than ever to win this trial.

The trial continued as it had kicked off, at lightning pace. There was plenty of back and forth between the two sides, resulting in a very even contest. The two presented valid arguments for both sides, using witnesses as well as submitted evidence. The breakthrough in the trial, however, came from Chloe.

"Ladies and gentlemen, item C."

A hospital bill was presented to the jury clearly showing the injuries and the cost of the injuries which Clifford had sustained from the alleged attack. Ross, panicked, desperately tried to find the bill in his notes but realised he must have left it at home in his rush. Chloe made the point that the injuries sustained weren't made by a lampshade as Clifford claimed; a doctor had confirmed that the injuries were likely not caused by human effect but by an accidental occurrence.

"Sidebar, your honour."

The judge was looking very tired, having already officiated at six trials that day.

"*What do you want?*"

"*Item C wasn't in the evidence list,*" Ross argued.

"*Yes, it was! It was declared ages ago by the guy before me!*"

"*Listen, Ross, if Chloe says it is, I'm not going to bother checking it. Just admit you'd forgotten it and cross argue. It's been a long day.*"

Chloe smirked at Ross again as they made their way back to their seats. Ross was sure he hadn't seen that piece of evidence before, but given the situation, it was entirely possible he had missed it. He stayed standing as he wanted to argue his case, but with no real evidence to prove his point, his argument was weak and poorly received by the jury. Looking to cut his losses, Ross rushed back to his seat.

"*Normally we would have closing remarks, but seeing where this is going, I'm just going to let the jury vote.*"

The jury exited through a door on the left as Ross gently thumped the table in front of him. He had choked it and, more importantly, lost to Chloe again. The jury were quick in their decision, returning in five minutes. The speaker took his stand and announced the verdict.

"*We, the jury, find the defendant, Maria Lemos…not guilty of domestic abuse and an account of assault.*"

The lecturer banged the gavel on the deck and Ross's head sank. Two defeats in a matter of 10 hours. The class was officially dismissed and the lecture theatre began to empty. Ross stared blankly at his notes for a moment while a smiling Chloe packed up her stuff. Then only Chloe, Ross and their lecturer remained.

"*Well done again, Ms Mitchener. Mr Susans, poor work missing out on a submitted piece of evidence. I expect better next time.*"

The lecturer left and Chloe headed to the exit.

"Chloe, wait," Ross called. She paused and turned around.

"What do you want Ross?"

"I just wanted to say well done." He stood up from his seat and walked toward her.

"You were never any competition."

Ross now stood face to face with his enemy from school The two were locked in a staring contest before Chloe broke the silence.

"You want anything in particular?"

"Not really, no."

"I'll be off then!"

As Chloe turned to go, Ross reached out and gripped her arm.

"Just one thing." He spun her round and pulled her in closer.

"What's that?"

"I don't lose anymore."

He leaned in toward her and kissed her passionately. He slammed her onto the table, the connection between them undeniable. The two were just getting started as the door swung open again and the sound of the janitor's bucket rattled through the lecture theatre. Chloe was quick to react and pushed Ross away from her, sending him flying over the table in front of him. The janitor popped his head around the door to see Chloe standing composed and Ross head over heels on a desk. He stared at them for a moment, shrugged his shoulders and continued listening to his music and mopping the floor.

Chloe grabbed her bag and made for the exit as Ross righted himself and followed behind her, calling her name. She ignored him. When he caught up to her, he forced her to speak to him.

"Why are you ignoring me?"

"That was a mistake."

"Then you might as well follow it all the way through." Ross smiled.

Several hours later, Ross and Chloe were lying naked in Chloe's bed. They had been for dinner and a short walk around Boston before coming back to Chloe's apartment. They started talking about how they had made it to Harvard. Chloe had gone to Stanford from school and had only recently transferred to Harvard for her final year. The two of them were having a surprisingly good time together. Ross turned to her with one more question.

"*So that Item C...*"

"*Yeah, what about it?*"

"*Does it actually exist? I swear I didn't see it.*"

Chloe started to laugh, putting down her glass of wine on a side table.

"*No, I made it up.*" She giggled.

"*I knew it!*" Ross screamed.

"*You got me!*"

"*How did you manage that?*"

"*When you have a certain reputation, as I do, it's important you use that to your advantage. I noticed you were tired as I walked in and still going through your notes. I knew you were unprepared. I also knew that Mrs Silicon is very impatient, so I knew she wouldn't question something I'd submitted as her top student.*"

Chloe smiled proudly as Ross lay in awe of her. Her attention to detail was incredible, and her ability to use her unique charm and eloquence was a thing to behold. Ross continued to stare at her as his phone began to ring. It was Jaz. The moment finally hit Ross: he was in bed with a girl, naked, less than 24 hours after he had thought his heart had been broken. He hid the phone from Chloe's view to avoid an awkward conversation. He declined the call and said it was an unknown number, probably sellers or something. His phone rang again, this time an unknown number. He told Chloe he had to take the call as it was about work. He threw on some boxers and stepped into the bathroom.

He picked up, ready to hear screaming or tears down the phone, but he was met with a very different message.

"You have a call from Boston Police Department. Would you like to accept?"

As the night drew to a close, Luke pulled past the LA sign. He had been driving for the better part of two hours since leaving the border, taking as many low-key roads as he could to avoid suspicion. He didn't want to be kicked out only hours after entering. He moved sensibly, sticking to the speed limit and not driving aggressively, contrary to his usual rash, reckless movements. He managed to complete the journey with relative ease, thinking only about Alejandro and getting him back as soon as possible. He had been given an address to go to via a text from Raquel. He was furious with her and still half-tempted to go after her, but he knew he had to bide his time until he had enough status to strike; it was certainly his long-term goal.

He cruised through the night version of Los Angeles, a unique place filled with a range of individuals from celebrities to drug dealers to both, certainly a land of opportunity if you were young and motivated as Luke was. He stuck to his rules as he drove past the police station, getting glares already from the cops standing outside. It may have been night, but this place never slept; bright lights illuminated the roads, emphasising the never-rest mentality of the place. After travelling through most of Los Angeles, his navigation system announced he had arrived at his location. Luke parked up and examined the house in front of him. Situated at the side of a mountain, it was composed of glass and other glossy materials, forming an exceptional piece of architecture. Luke was stunned as he stepped out the vehicle but also convinced he had the wrong address. Nevertheless, he approached the door.

Luke triple-checked the address and emerged from the shadows, stepping into the light and knocking on the door to the tune of Happy Birthday as he had been instructed to. He waited for a second before a lock clicked in the door and it swung open. Luke peeked round the door. The inside light was on, but he couldn't see anyone. He was about to call out when a young man walked through the hallway, munching on crisps. He stopped and stared at Luke. The young individual was barefoot, with perfectly parted hair, deep blue eyes and a noticeably built body. Luke stepped inside as the young man continued to stare at him, still munching on his Cheetos.

"Are you Noah?"

"No… I'm Jason, who are you?"

"I'm Luke. Raquel sent me."

"Oh, Raquel… I'm sorry, you're looking for Tommy."

"Could you go get him for me?"

"Sure. Come in. Take your shoes off."

Luke obliged. The theme of the colourful entrance was continued into the gigantic living room. The place was decorated like a nursery and, from what he could tell, run by 17-year-olds. Luke was convinced Raquel was playing a prank on him as he sat on the bright green sofa. He felt massively out of place in his dirty, tired black jacket and jeans. He waited awkwardly to find out what he was actually involved in here.

Jason returned with Tommy. Like Jason, Tommy was built like a model, with luxuriant blonde hair and piercing blue eyes, various tattoos and a few piercings to complete the look. Luke's confusion peaked; both of these boys looked no older than 18. Tommy introduced himself to Luke before telling Jason to go away. He took a seat opposite Luke on a yellow sofa.

"*What the fuck is this?*" Luke snapped.

"*Luke, calm down. I'll explain.*"

"*This looks like a fucking nursery, and you look like you work for Hollister!*"

"*Luke, calm down.*"

"*You look like you just popped out your mum's stomach, you twat, telling me to calm down.*"

"*Luke.*"

"*I bet you're a faggot as well, ain't ya?*

"*Luke! Listen. Let me explain.*"

"*Go on then, you faggot.*"

"*This isn't a trap house; it's an influencer house. We're all influencers on social media.*"

"*What the fuck?*"

"*Luke, listen —*"

"*No bruv I —*"

Luke was interrupted by some laughs from across the house.

"*Who the fuck is laughing?*"

"*Who the fuck says bruv, dude?*" the distant voice shouted.

Luke stared back at Tommy, astonished at what he was witnessing. He paused a second before storming up to where the comment had come from, locating Jason who was still eating his crisps. He choked as he saw the large frame of Luke marching toward him. Luke dashed his crisps to one side before pinning him against a wall and slamming his arm into his neck. Tommy rushed over to stop the commotion, with more members of the house converging on the incident. Tommy pulled Luke away from Jason, urging the other boys away as well. Jason stared at Luke with fear in his eyes as Luke smiled back at him. Tommy led Luke back down to the living area and explained further.

"Listen, Luke, this is unconventional, but it works. There are 17 of us in this house, me included, and we make up the internet group called PSYCHY. We have 14 million followers across many platforms and do stuff like stunts, pranks and other funny videos."

"I don't care about your fucking group. Why am I here?"

"The group is a front for Raquel and her drug business."

"What?"

"Yeah, we run it. No one questions it because of apparent internet fame. Everyone just expects us to live in this kind of house and have the kind of money we do."

"I don't believe this – you're 17!"

"18, actually. We run it effectively and have been very successful."

"This is a joke!"

Luke went to march out of the house, but Tommy got up and slowed him down.

"Listen, I know it's not conventional."

"Conventional? This is fucking stupid, bruv!"

"Trust me, give it a week."

"Why should I?"

"I think you would want to see the amount of money you can earn."

Luke realised he was acting irrationally; he had to get Raquel and remembered his end goal, so he decided to bite the bullet, as hard as it was. He instructed Tommy to show him where he was staying. Tommy led him through the house, which became more and more ridiculous as they travelled through it. The walls were lined with photos of different members of the group, all of whom were male. The house had only colourful seating combined with random decorations dotted around and a speaker constantly blasting out alternative music Luke could not decipher. It felt as if he was in a different generation.

They managed to travel through the jungle of the house to Luke's makeshift room. He walked into another very brightly coloured room, this time with LED lights and lava lamps to add to the effect. The room was huge and topped off with a king-size bed, as well as a walk-in wardrobe and an impressive gaming set-up, including a 70-inch mounted tv. Luke's face dropped as Tommy showed him the room; he couldn't believe what he was experiencing. He had been used to the smaller, more secret operations of London, which were always run on a tight budget and demanded a life lived on the edge, but these boys were both living a life of luxury and hiding in plain sight.

Luke dragged his suitcase in and sat on the desk of the gaming set-up. Tommy stood at the doorway asking if he needed anything.

"When do we get to work?"

"We'll start in the morning. It's 2 am."

Luke acknowledged the time as Tommy took off, closing the door behind him. He had a million questions. He was about to ring Raquel and express his anger but remembered the time and decided to get some sleep, especially after all he had been through in the past 24 hours.

The sun glistened through Luke's large window; he had been too tired to shut the electric blinds the day before. He got up grumpily and went to close the blinds. He collapsed back onto the bed and had just hit the mattress when he heard a scream from outside. Alarmed, he jumped up and grabbed his gun from his suitcase. He peeked out of his door and saw no one in the corridor. He was about to step out when he heard another scream coming from the entrance. He crept out of his room and carefully headed in the direction of the scream. At the corner, he noticed a splash of blood on the floor. He took a deep breath, rolled round the corner and fixed his aim down the hallway. He had hardly adjusted his eyes when a splurge of red liquid was dashed across his face. He dropped his gun and let out a yell, which was met by a bunch of laughs.

Luke opened his eyes to discover he was covered in what appeared to be a mix of sauces producing a horrid smell. Tommy face palmed as he quickly went to help Luke, bringing a towel and explaining that they were filming a prank, firing sauces at random members of the house as they walked past. Luke was furious and shouted at Tommy as he went back to his room to have a shower. He knew it was going to be a challenge for him to bite his tongue through all this.

"Yes, I'll accept the call."

"Putting you through now."

Ross was expecting another call from Jaz but had no idea who would call him from the police station.

"Hello?" came a meek voice.

"Yeah, who's this?"

"Ross! Oh my god, thank you for picking up!"

"Who is this?"

"It's Tyler."

Ross rolled his eyes. He and Tyler had fallen out just as he and Jaz were looking to move in together. Tyler had warned Ross about gossip he had heard about her, but Ross claimed he was merely jealous, and the pair grew apart.

"Tyler? Why the fuck are you calling me from the police station?"

"I'm in some trouble. I need help."

Ross sighed. He hadn't talked to him in a while, but throughout his Harvard experience, Tyler had been the only one who'd been there for him and he could always trust him. He said he would be down there as soon as he could.

As he stepped out of the bathroom, he was met with Chloe's eyes fixed on his body. He started to gather his clothes, and Chloe asked what he was doing.

"*A mate of mine's in trouble and needs some help.*"

"*Who? What's the trouble?*"

"*I must move,*" said Ross, throwing on his shoes before dashing out of the room.

"*Wait!*" Chloe called out after him. "*I don't have your number!*"

Ross was already out of earshot, his mind racing as to what Tyler would have done. Tyler was one of the most peaceful and harmless people he had ever met and would never step a foot out of line. Shaking the thought away, he parked outside the police station and stepped out into the Boston night.

Ross blinked as he entered the brightly lit station and went over to the desk.

"*Hey, I'm here to pay for Tyler Sampson's bail.*"

"*Sit there.*"

The staff member pointed to a group of chairs that looked as crooked as the rest of the building. Ross took a seat and waited to be called. The night staff was always slower, especially in a police station. Eventually, Tyler was brought out in handcuffs. Ross stood up and went over to the desk.

"*$1500 please, sir.*"

Ross reluctantly gave over his card before turning to Tyler, who could only look at the floor. Confused, Ross typed in his pin and was given his receipt, and Tyler was freed from his handcuffs and handed over to Ross, who escorted him out. In silence, they got into Ross's car.

"*So what happened, Tyler?*"

No reply.

"*Well?*"

He remained silent, still looking at the floor.

"*Tyler!*" Ross shouted.

"*Ok man! They caught me with some shit.*"

"*What shit?*"

"Just some stuff."

"What fucking stuff, Tyler? Drug stuff?"

"Yeah," he whispered.

"What did you say?"

"Yes."

"I can't hear you."

"Yes, ok! They caught me and a few other guys with drugs."

"You fucking idiot."

"Ross man, listen. Get off your high horse. Everyone does it."

"My high horse? Did you not listen to a single word I told you about my brother?"

"It's different, man."

"Get out."

"What?"

"Get the fuck out of my car."

"Okay bro."

"Don't call me bro, and you owe me $1500."

"Bro."

"Get the fuck out!"

"Okay man."

Tyler stepped out of the car and closed the door behind him. Ross rolled the window down.

"You changed bro," Ross said calmly.

"I haven't, you have."

"Oh yeah, how many people know you're bi? Or is that too much of an embarrassment for you to admit to now, Mr Alpha Male?"

"Oh, that's how we're doing it."

"Yes, you prick."

"In that case, how's Jazmine?"

"You fucking dickhead."

Ross stepped out of the car and went round to square up against Tyler. The two were inches apart until Ross noticed a few policemen staring in their direction. He took a step back, still keeping eye contact with Tyler until he stepped into his car. He put up his middle finger in his direction as he rolled up the window and pulled off with speed, to the visible displeasure of the onlooking officers. Tyler stared at him as he drove away, then casually left the police station.

As Ross took off down the highway, the events of the last 48 hours hit him. He had broken up with the apparent love of his life, had sex with an old enemy from school and had now lost a friend the same way he had lost his brother. He slammed the steering wheel in frustration.

Wearily, he parked outside his apartment and made his way to the stairs As he checked his pocket for his key, he heard a movement on the steps. He looked up to see Jaz sitting there with tears in her eyes.

She still looked beautiful to him, even in tears and after what she had done to him. The two continued to stare at each other until Jaz raised a hand to wave at him. After a moment, Ross did the same.

"*Hey,*" Jaz said softly.

"*Hey,*" Ross whispered back.

"*How are you?*"

"*How am I?*" Ross chuckled.

"*Yeah.*"

"*Shit. What about you?*"

"*Even worse.*"

"*Really?*" Ross said, surprised.

"*Yes, I miss you so much already. It was such a big mistake. I didn't mean it at all. It was just something that happened in the moment, you know. I was drunk, and I didn't know what was happening, and I am just so sorry.*"

"*Wow.*"

"Yes, Ross! I'm yours. I love you."

Ross was about to speak, a slight smile appearing on his face, when he heard another sound. From the shadows emerged a short blonde with piercing blue eyes. Chloe. The smile quickly disappeared from Ross's face.

"You forgot to get my number. I thought I'd come and see you."

"Uh, Ross. Who the fuck is that?" Jaz snapped.

"I'm Chloe. Who are you?"

"Jaz, his girlfriend, bitch."

"Ross, you have a fucking girlfriend! What the fuck? Why did you sleep with me?"

"You slept with her? We were broken up for one day!"

Ross tried to get a word in, but now their combined aggression was toward him and he couldn't speak without being screamed out.

"Sleep somewhere else tonight!" Jaz yelled and left.

"Fuck you, prick!" Chloe shouted before storming off down the street.

Ross stood flailing his arms in frustration.

"Fuck!" he screamed, marching back to his car and taking off down the road again.

4th July 2027

Luke sat in the PSYCHY living room, looking at the gorgeous view provided by a mountain-side house. He had been based at PSYCHY for nearly three years, having had multiple run-ins with other groups and acting very much as a fixer for PSYCHY. The members of the group had chopped and changed, but the core members, Jason, Elijah, Tommy, Dan and Luke, had stayed. Over time, Luke became the boss of the group. Their operation was efficient as Luke had years of experience over the others and it kept working for him. He raised a glass of whiskey as he watched the sun set on another day at the top of the pile. It was also the biggest day in three years for Luke: the release of Alejandro.

For months when Luke started out, he was promised Alejandro. Raquel kept him as motivation until Luke had paid off his debt to her. This time was now. The plan was for Alejandro to be dropped off at the airport where Luke would collect him, and he would be done with Raquel and be able to go and run his own business. Luke had bitten his tongue and showed patience for once in his life. He had not reacted to any of the hurdles that had been thrown in his way. Today was the day he escaped all of that. He finished off his whiskey, grabbed his jacket and strolled to his car, a brand-new all-blacked Mustang that mirrored his own hardness and sense of security. He pulled off the driveway and made his way toward LAX. Borderline by Tame Impala began to play on the radio as he drove across Los Angeles.

After 25 minutes, he pulled up in the LAX car park, now listening to King's Dead. A total mood change. Luke parked the car and waited. His instructions had been texted to him by Raquel. He was to wait for a call from her when Alejandro had been delivered to the airport. When his phone rang, it was an incoming Facetime call from Raquel. Luke quickly picked up. His screen buffered for a second before he met face to face with Raquel for the first time in years.

"*Hola, Luke.*"

"*Hola.*"

"*He's at LAX. You can go and get him.*"

"*Thank you, Raquel. Why the Facetime call?*"

"*Oh, I just wanted to see the look on your face.*"

"*Okay?*"

"*Have fun.*"

"*Bye, Raquel.*"

"*Oh, one second – I forgot!*"

"*Forgot what?*"

"*Alejandro is here with me!*"

"*What?*"

Raquel spun the camera around to show a tearful Alejandro with multiple bruises across his bare body and a gag in his mouth.

"*Raquel! What the fuck?*"

"*This is your fault, Luke.*"

"*What the fuck, you fucking bitch? I did everything you asked me to!*"

"*You think I don't know about the money you've been stealing?*"

"*I wasn't stealing it. It was for Alejandro when he got here so he could start a life away from all this, go and make something of himself.*"

"*You stole from me.*"

"*I didn't fucking steal from you! Untie him!*"

"*As you wish.*"

Raquel instructed one of the masked men to untie Alejandro and remove the gag from his mouth.

"*Luke!*" cried Alejandro.

"*Alejandro! I'm here, I'm gonna get you out.*"

"*Oh, you shouldn't tell lies, Luke,*" said Raquel.

"*Raquel, let him go.*"

"*Oh, I will… to heaven.*"

"*Raquel, no!*"

Raquel let off three shots into Alejandro's chest and forehead. She chuckled as his body went limp before draping across the floor. After a minute Luke stopped screaming and sat in silence, which was more ominous. He held a deathly stare at the screen as Raquel flipped it to her face.

"*Oh, why so glum?*"

"*You think I'm gonna work for you after this?*"

"Oh Luke, I never expected you to anyway. You're aged. You're dispensable."

"What?"

"You're finished, Luke."

"What?"

"Have fun!" And Raquel ended the call.

Luke realised Raquel knew exactly where he was and could easily have men around everywhere. He sat upright and was about to slam down the accelerator when a bullet smashed into his rear-view mirror. After the initial shock, Luke sped away from the airport, hearing a few more shots come whistling past his car.

He had to get back to the PSYCHY house quickly now that Raquel had made him a target. He sped through the main streets of Los Angeles, even running a few red lights, and spun the car into the driveway. He noted none of the others' cars were there so he must have beaten them. He cracked the door open and found the lights were off. He had left them on.

"Yo!" he called a few times, to no response, and took a few steps in.

"Flash out!"

Luke was blinded by a bright surge of energy erupting from the flash grenade. A sea of voices converged on him.

"Get down! Police!"

They forced Luke to the ground as he cupped his ears in pain The room was spinning around him. A firm pair of hands fastened his arms behind his back before applying ice-cold handcuffs that pinched his skin.

He stayed pretty nauseous as the police escorted him to the police car. Through his blurry vision, all he could see was Raquel smoking a cigarette in the distance, with the rest of the house looking on. He gave Raquel one final stare before a policeman forced him into the car and slammed the door behind him.

He sat, dazed, in the police car as the officer drove him to the LAPD headquarters in the centre of LA. He was dragged out of the car and hauled into the station. The officer walked to his desk, and Luke took a seat in the empty seating area, patiently waiting to be called. His hands were still cuffed and his mouth was dry, but his vision was returning.

The officer hauled him up again and dragged him toward the first interrogation room. He shoved Luke through the door, threw him against the table and slammed the door behind him.

"*Easy!*" commanded the detective.

Luke stumbled onto the chair before examining the individual in front of him. He sat looking up at Detective Asrhin Khalef, originally from Pakistan. The detective sported a moustache and long black hair with a classic side parting. A cup of hot coffee was clasped firmly in his hands. The detective stared back down at him with a smile and an air of mystery. Flicking his hair from side to side, as he took a seat opposite Luke and placed his coffee on the wobbly table.

"*Mr Luke Moffat!*"

"*Yes...*" Luke whispered.

"*We've been watching you.*"

"*No clue what you're on about.*"

"*Don't play dumb, Luke. We know everything. We know about Raquel; we know about the border and we know about her drug operation. Here's the good news: you get to help us! She wanted you dead, I saved you.*"

"*Still don't know what you're talking about.*"

"*Come on, Luke, give it up. If you help me get Raquel, I'll get your charges dropped.*"

"*Who's Raquel?*"

The inspector scoffed before sitting back in his seat, his eyes still on Luke's face. Luke remained calm; it was nothing he hadn't been through before. The detective folded his arms and continued to probe.

"Luke, you're facing serious time if you don't cooperate. We've got you on suspicion of drug possession, intent to deal, dealing and even assault. Don't be silly now."

"I don't know what you're talking about. I would like to speak to a lawyer."

"Oh, of course."

"Could I have a phone then please, bruv?"

"No."

"What the fuck?"

"You're gonna tell me what I need to know."

"I don't know no Raquel man. Piss off!"

"Go get him a phone," the detective instructed the officer.

"Thank you."

"After this phone call, you better be talking because even if I let you go, Raquel wants you dead."

The detective pushed away from the table and followed the officer out of the room, leaving Luke alone in the interrogation room. This gave him a moment to collect his thoughts and examine the room. It was a typical holding cell with dull grey walls, a tiny viewing window, and a camera in the corner. The poor-quality furniture made the place look even shabbier. He sat upright in his chair, waiting for his phone. This is when it dawned on him that he had no one to call as Alejandro was dead.

The officer returned, gave Luke his phone back and released him from the handcuffs. Luke unlocked his phone and scrolled through his contact list, desperately wondering who to call and, more importantly, who would actually help. He arrived at a contact, possibly the only person that would pick up for sure. He dialled the number. After a few rings, Luke breathed a sigh of relief as a woman's voice echoed down the phone.

"Hello? Who's this?"

"Hey, Geo."

Georgia hesitated for a solid few seconds before replying.

"Luke. What do you want?"

"I need your help, Geo. I fucked up."

"Don't call me Geo. It's Georgia. And Luke, you've fucked up enough times."

"Geo. Please!"

"What do you need?"

"$10,000."

"Luke, what the fuck!"

"I can fight this, Geo. I'm innocent."

"Innocent?"

"Yes."

"Were you still innocent when I was raped?"

Luke was silent.

"Or what about when mum got killed?"

Silence again.

"Or when you killed Bilal?"

"Ok! I get it."

"You're sick."

"Geo, please. I'm innocent."

Georgia stayed silent for a minute or so, leaving Luke to speculate on his future. This was a huge moment for him; if he was posted on bail, he would be able to get a lawyer to fight his case and protect himself as much as possible while also going for Raquel.

"Ok."

"Ok?"

"I'll do it, but you have to pay me back, with interest!"

"Yeah, calm. Say you're my lawyer and you're posting bail."

"Say I'm your what?"

Luke called for the guard and shoved the phone in his face, forcing Georgia to speak to him. The guard marched off with the phone as Luke sighed with relief. His sister had always been by his side, even after what had happened to her as a result of his actions. He sat fumbling with his thumbs as he waited for the guard to return. Distant footsteps re-alerted his focus and he sat upright in the metal chair. The guard pulled him out of the chair and escorted him down the corridor to the front desk.

"Mr Moffat?"

"Yeah."

"You've been granted bail, paid by your lawyer."

"Thank you."

"Your bail relies on five conditions, most notably not to flee or to talk to anyone with a police record."

"Anything else?"

"Be careful, Mr Moffat."

"Always."

Luke collected his things packed into an envelope from the reception lady before strolling out through the front door, drawing a few eyeballs from the officers who had brought him in. For now, he was free, but he needed to find representation as soon as possible.

He had no idea where to begin until he stood opposite one of the subway entrances. He crossed the street, keeping an eye on his surroundings. Raquel would surely have men on him almost constantly. He walked down the subway stairs with no intention of going on any of the trains; he was looking for a newspaper stand. He found one adjacent to the ticket office. The man looked up at him and smiled. Luke stared back at him, feeling slightly confused.

"You got any newspapers bruv?"

"Yes sir, over there!" the owner replied with an accent. Luke picked up a few, scanning through them. He was looking for a story about a court case in which a lawyer had proved innocence. There! A New York lawyer had proved the innocence of a notorious gang member after he'd been accused of drug dealing. The gang member, also a basketball player, had been accused of dealing in small amounts to his teammates, but his lawyer managed to get him off every single charge. The lawyer was also in another story, having become the youngest junior partner in his firm's history due to his 100% success rate with his cases so far. Luke noted the lawyer's name and hurried off. The owner called out to him, but Luke paid no attention as he left the subway station and returned to the street. As his signal returned, he dialled the firm's number which he had obtained from their website. The phone rang a few times before someone picked up.

"*Good morning, you're through to Walker Malcolm Law Firm. How may I help you today?*"

"*I need a lawyer.*"

"*Are you a client?*"

"*No, but –*"

"*I'm sorry, sir, but if you want to join as a client you'll need to come here in person.*"

"*I can't, it's an ongoing case. I'm only out on bail.*"

"*Sorry, sir, you would still have to come here.*"

"*Fuck, ok, I'll be there tomorrow.*"

Luke hung up the phone and walked with more direction toward the bank. He had a special savings account which he had set up for if he ever desperately needed money, but he had to move quickly as the threat from Raquel also loomed large, with the chances of her striking increasing by the second. At the bank, he waited at the back of the queue which stretched out nearly to the entrance. He scanned the room looking for exits and possible threats; this was almost second nature to Luke now. When Luke stood next in line, a slot opened up on the right and Luke was called over by a familiar voice. Luke walked to the till and was met by the owner of the newsstand. He stared at the man who carried the same accent as before.

"What can I do for you, sir?"

"Do you not remember me?"

"Not at all, sir."

"Never mind, I need to take some money out."

"There is an ATM outside sir."

"Yeah, this is kind of a large amount."

Luke leant in closer to the man who appeared to have duplicated. He explained that he needed $15,000 and they had to be as quiet as possible. The man understood and called up Luke's account number. He said he had to check this amount with his manager and went off to the back office. A man emerged and came to serve Luke, but it wasn't the man who had served him at first.

"Where's the other don?"

"Excuse me, sir?"

His voice was different as well. He was now a pale, ginger assistant who looked as though he was still in high school.

"The other guy who was serving me."

"It's only been me, sir. I have your 15."

"Oh yes, sorry."

The new assistant lead him through to the side of the bank where he could collect his money. On the short walk, he stared at the assistant and looked around for the other man he had seen here and at the newsstand.

"Everything ok, sir?"

"Yes, sorry. Where's the money?"

"Right here, sir."

The ginger lad handed him a sealed bag with a label on it. Luke snatched the bag and hid it in his rucksack out of public sight. He thanked the attendant and walked out of the bank. He made his way back to the subway to get to LAX as quickly as possible. Once down the stairs, he walked towards the newsstand and through the crowd of bodies saw the man serving a customer. However, when he reached the newsstand, it was deserted. He did a 360 spin looking for the man, before shaking his head and walking away down the subway. Taking one last look at the newsstand, he saw the man was sitting there looking at him. He chose to ignore it on this occasion and focussed on getting to LAX.

The train journey was uneventful. He had been expecting an early move from Raquel, but he hadn't noted any suspicious individuals following him so far. At LAX, he hopped off the train and went to the ticket office. Luke was thankful to see a woman server instead of the man he had been seeing. He bought a $150 ticket to New York, and as he had no baggage to book, he went straight through to security. He suddenly realised he had just under $15,000 stashed in his bag when the maximum allowed was $10,000. He knew he didn't have time to sort it out; his flight left in 45 minutes. He smiled at the security attendant as he emptied his rucksack into the plastic tray, throwing the rucksack with the money in it into the tray as well. It went onto the electric conveyor as Luke was asked to step through the security gate. He was cleared by the attendant, who ushered him round to collect his things.

He discovered his tray had been moved into the search pile. He was called round by the attendant, whose voice he again recognised. There was the man he had seen at the newsstand and the bank.

"*Who the fuck are you?*" he blurted out.

His little explosion drew the gaze of onlookers, which calmed Luke down. He had to move in silence or risk being caught violating the rules of his parole. He composed himself before trying again.

"*Sorry, what's the problem with the bag?*"

The attendant pulled out a pocketknife that Luke had forgotten about. Eager to get through the gate as soon as possible, Luke said he could confiscate it. The attendant removed the pocketknife and handed the bag back to Luke, paying no attention to the money. He appeared to have got away with it, and he grabbed the bag, but the attendant held onto it.

"Be careful, Luke," he whispered.

"What the fuck?"

"Your ticket fell, sir."

Luke looked up from the bag to see a different individual, this time pale with frizzy brown hair and a dated moustache. He stared at the attendant, convinced he had seen the man from the newsstand and the bank before.

"Sir?" the attendant asked.

"Sorry, thanks."

Luke grabbed his ticket from the attendant's hand and shot off toward the terminal from which he would soon be taking off to New York. He was desperately trying to establish whether the man he had been seeing was even real. Was he a person he knew, or perhaps a man whom Raquel had sent after him? His thoughts were cut short as he noticed a number of police and security guards posted at the majority of the gates. He had to move quickly.

He navigated his way through the centre of the airport, surrounded by duty-free shops looking to scam the general public, as well as fast-food chains looking to poison them. He kept a low profile and didn't speak to anyone until he reached his gate. The plane was already boarding, but he took a seat until his section was called. He completed his routine room check and didn't notice anything suspicious. He remained confident about this until two men strolled in dressed in jackets and dark shades and took a seat directly behind Luke. They began to talk loudly so that Luke could hear their conversation; he could not help but listen in. They were talking in Spanish, and from what Luke could gather, they were talking about returning to Mexico, which was strange as they were in boarding for a flight to New York. Despite his suspicions, Luke chose to remain calm and patient.

When his seat row was called, he stood up carefully, clutching his rucksack firmly, assuming that was what they were after. He joined the queue to get onto the plane, aware that they hadn't followed him. He was so focussed on them that the attendant had to call him twice when he reached the front of the queue. He handed over his ticket and passport, and the attendant tore his ticket and let him through. He exhaled as he passed through the gate. Neither of the men had moved, and he seemed to have got to the plane unscathed.

He went through into the main cabin of the plane, the flight attendant directing him to his seat which was a window seat halfway down the plane. He kept his rucksack with him to ensure it was safe and settled down. As he got comfortable, he heard the same voices he'd heard behind him at the gate. He cautiously raised his head and looked in the direction of the voices; sure enough, the two men were seated three rows in front of him on the right. He shrank down and lay back in his chair. The plane filled up quickly, with Luke placed next to an engaged couple.

"*Hey, how are you!*"

Luke looked the couple up and down before shaking his head.

"*Bit rude that.*"

"*Shut up, love.*"

"*Oi, watch how you speak to my wife!*"

Luke started chuckling.

"*What's so fucking funny?*"

"*Who says oi, bruv? We're in LA.*"

"*Listen, you little maggot.*"

"Sorry, ok."

"Good."

The two took their seats, the wife sitting between the men to prevent any further tension. The four-hour flight could not have gone slower, and Luke decided to take a nap. As he awoke, the plane began to descend and landed at New York International Airport.

The couple next to Luke moved into the aisle and Luke followed suit, watching for the two men who had somehow made it onto the flight before him, but he couldn't locate them in the crowd. The passengers slowly disembarked, and Luke stuck to the crowd as they filled the terminal.

With no baggage to collect, Luke went straight toward the exit. The working day was coming to an end, so he stepped out into rush hour in the Big Apple. He had told the receptionist that he would arrive the following day, but he was anxious to sort out representation as soon as possible, so he jumped into the first cab he saw outside the airport and gave the driver directions. As the taxi took off, he looked around for the men he had seen on the plane, but they were nowhere in sight. Luke assumed he had lost them in the crush and relaxed in the back seat of the taxi.

New York was even more built-up than Central LA. Luke looked like a typical tourist as he stared out of the window at the mammoth skyscrapers occupying the city skyline. When the taxi arrived at the law firm, Luke threw $10 in the front seat, instructing the driver to keep the change, as he stepped out and looked up at the gigantic building in front of him. The trail of suits constantly exiting and entering the building contrasted with Luke's simple attire of air forces and bomber jacket, a British staple. After his initial awe, he made his way into the building, which had 73 floors in total. He needed to go to the very top.

He approached the front desk, noticing that a pass was required to get past security to get into the elevator. He explained to the receptionist that he had a meeting with Sam Walker of Walker and Malcolm. The receptionist didn't ask him many questions and handed him a pass with the name Harry Barnes, probably another one of Sam Walker's clients. He flashed his security pass to the guard before getting into the elevator headed toward the 73rd floor. The elevator music deafened him.

The ding was a blessing to his ears as the doors popped open and Luke stepped out, still clutching his rucksack and looking seriously out of place among the posh offices filled with smartly dressed people. He kissed his teeth at anyone who stared at him. He noticed security was also on this level, so he continued to move with caution. He approached the receptionist, who was more focused on her screen than on Luke addressing her.

"Excuse me."

"One second, sir."

Luke took a step back from the desk and did his scan of the room. The eyes of security were on him, probably because of his attire. The other security guard had moved position, and Luke was unaware of where he had gone.

"Yes, sir."

"I'm looking to become a client."

"Of course, sir. What's the business?"

"No business, it's a personal issue."

"I'm afraid we don't really do those cases, sir."

"What about this then?"

Luke placed the newspaper article he had found in front of the receptionist, pointing to the name of the lawyer on the case.

"Sam Walker – I want to speak to him."

"He won't speak to you, sir."

"Listen you little bitch, let me speak to him. It's urgent."

As he raised his voice, the security walked toward him and the other one appeared out of nowhere on his left. The two guards converged on him and grabbed him under the arms before forcing him down to the floor and tying his hands behind his back. Luke screamed to be let go, causing a crowd to gather in reception. Eventually, a voice drowned out the others as even Sam Walker was drawn out of his office, calling for people to go back to work and approaching the security guards.

"What are you doing?"

"This man was causing trouble, sir."

"Trouble? He's in a bomber jacket, for God's sake. Get him up."

"But sir —"

"What does he want?"

"A lawyer."

"Send him to my office."

"But sir —"

"No arguments."

Sam spun around and returned to his office. In a matter of minutes, he had diffused a difficult situation. Sam was a charmer and a problem solver, a relentless winner who never turned down a challenge. He paid special attention to cases that seemed a bit shady, and Luke had that particular aura about him.

Luke was helped to his feet, released from handcuffs and escorted to Sam's office. The room was huge and occupied the corner of the office with the best view. It was encased in sparkling glass and housed an impressive bookcase filled with reference works and leather-bound journals. Luke scanned the room in amazement, this time, rather than to check for danger and finally took a seat.

"So, Luke."

"Yeah."

"What's the problem?"

"You did this, right?" Luke referred to the news article again.

"*That wasn't me, no.*"

"*What? It says Walker and Malcolm.*"

"*Yes, the firm Walker and Malcolm.*"

"*Who did it then?*"

"*There he is now.*"

Sam's gaze caused Luke to spin around in his chair. A Rolls Royce of a man strolled through the lobby. He had jet black hair with a beard cut to perfection and the swagger of a jazz band. The man turned sharply and came into the office. His suit was as sharp as his beard, and his eyes carried a strange weight. He took a few elegant strides forward. The man looked more like a model than a lawyer and was surely a heartbreaker. Luke looked him up and down as he pulled up a seat next to him, focused on his eyes, the only part of him that seemed to be flawed.

"*Who are you bruv?*"

"*No need to be so aggressive, Luke. Introduce yourself.*"

"*Who are you?*" the man enquired.

"*I asked first bruv.*"

"*If you want my help, you'll tell me first.*"

"*Fine, fucking hell, man. I'm Luke.*"

"*Full name?*"

"*Jesus Christ! It's Luke fucking Moffat.*"

"*Have to be thorough with these things.*"

"*Shut up man. Who are you?*"

"*Interesting middle name as well; I haven't heard Fucking before.*"

"*Bruv!*"

"*Calm down.*"

"*Stop messing around. Who are you?*"

"*My name is Ross, Ross Susans.*"

A 25-year-old Ross Susans sat at the desk of his brand-new office, furnished to the max. He had graduated from Harvard two years ago and was handpicked by Sam Walker to work at his firm after impressing him in numerous mock trials, as well as finishing top of his class in all but one of his subjects. Sam had brought Ross in with a view of one day making him a name partner in the firm. Ross was meeting expectations, if not exceeding them, and had become the youngest junior partner in the firm's history.

Ross was currently wrapped up in a drug case involving a local gang member. The case was widely reported across the country as the young prodigy freeing the rich again and not holding them accountable for their actions. However, only Ross knew the true story. He had been assigned the case as a simple misdemeanour as the firm did not know the backstory of the client very well. On the day he went to visit the man, named Lukas, he found him torturing a man for information. Ross was willing to let the case go, but Lukas threatened him, saying he had to represent him or he would kill him. He was not to tell anyone about his actions; he was protected in all aspects of the law. When Lukas got caught again, it was flagged up to a judge, and the case went to trial. It made Ross sick to the stomach that he had to defend a man who was involved in such activities, particularly considering his brother's history and drug abuse. Nevertheless, he had no choice but to do it, and do it successfully or risk death. Sam continued to praise him for his work, but the reality was Ross was even questioning his own morals and integrity.

The more the case went on, the more Ross lost himself. His physical exterior appeared strong and masked the mush of emotions he experienced on a daily basis; despite getting to where he had always wanted to be, his mind was in a place he had never thought it would be. For years, he had ignored all his childhood trauma, and it had finally caught up with him. But he had to keep it buried; he wasn't at his final goal yet, and any sign of weakness in the professional world gets leapt on, so it was important to him to keep up a tough exterior. This is how Ross had been for the last three years. He didn't let anyone in and didn't trust anyone at all.

After the Jazmine and Chloe debacle, Ross struggled to maintain any long-term relationships, opting for casual hook-ups. Jaz had ruined his perception of long-term love, and Chloe, being touch and go, was a reminder of Jaz as well. He couldn't deal with that sort of pain anymore and decided not to develop long-lasting relationships or friendships. He was scared of being left alone as, in his mind, everyone leaves.

Today, Ross was looking at the reaction to his winning the Lukas drug case. As much as it had distressed him, it showed the level of lawyer he was as the odds were heavily stacked against him. The office had been given to him weeks before, but now he felt as though he had really earned it, especially because of his new title, junior partner. Sam had chosen him as his vote. The two had a special relationship; although Ross had problems maintaining friendships, he saw Sam as his mentor and possibly the only person he could trust. Sam saw Ross in the same way, as his student to whom he could pass on his knowledge.

Ross had overseen 53 cases in his two years at the firm and hadn't lost a case; he'd had no losses at all at trial and the rest were settlements. He would use his charm, eloquence and negotiating skills to win every time. If you were in a jam, he was your man, for sure. This fixer persona Ross had created had become popular with celebrities, and many clients from Hollywood asked him to get them out of their issues, normally domestic arguments or petty crime charges. Ross had always set the rule he wouldn't do drug cases until Lukas forced him to.

Ross had set out wanting to help people, but he lost himself somewhere in the world of money, status and success. It had cost him his happiness and his sanity, but he couldn't show an inch of that to the outside world. He stared at the newspaper which had branded him the rich man's maid, listing multiple celebrities he had got off charges of illegal activities. He was stuck in a loop, and there was no way out; if he rejected a case, Sam would fire him for letting easy money go.

Ross had received a few emails, though, including one stating that there would be a potential client flying in from LA., which piqued his interest. Up till now, he had been doing individual work, but this could be his chance to land his first client on his first day as junior partner. As he read through his emails, his work phone rang.

"Hello, Sunny?"

"Hi sir, Mr Reid is through to see you in conference room C."

"Already? Oh, for God's sake. Thank you, Sunny."

"No worries, sir."

Sunny had been Ross's secretary since his first day at the firm. She had initially been an intern, but Ross had insisted they keep her on as he liked her style and work ethic. The two had a strong professional relationship, but Ross let her know little about his personal life, no matter how hard she pressed. He pushed away from his desk and made his way over to see Mr Reid in conference room C.

Mr Reid was one of Ross's ongoing cases. A self-made millionaire, Alex Reid had been cheating on his wife and was worried she was going to find out. He had come to Ross, who knew his reputation, and once more, Ross had been forced to take his case. He had hired a private investigator to see whether

Mr Reid was at risk of being caught, but he had turned up without an appointment, so it must be an emergency.

When Ross strolled into the conference room, he was greeted by Mr Reid, who was pacing around the room.

"What the fuck did you do?"

"What the fuck did I do?"

"She found out Ross! She knows everything."

"That's your fault."

"You're my lawyer – you're meant to make it go away!"

"How about you don't cheat in the first place?"

"What did you say to me."

"Just a thought."

Their attention was diverted by screaming coming from the main lobby just outside the elevator, but Mr Reid continued his rambling complaints.

"Get out of my sight."

"These are our offices." Ross chuckled.

"Fine! I'll go and you won't be hearing from me again!"

"No worries, Mr Reid."

Ross happily waved him off as he stormed out, huffing and puffing. Ross followed him down to the lobby, where everything seemed fairly normal.

"Sunny! What happened?"

"Some man came in, started a scene."

"Where is he?"

"Sam took him into his office."

"What, why?"

"He said he needed a lawyer."

Ross observed that she was wearing a noticeably tight dress and had slightly changed her hairstyle. He looked at her briefly again before making his way to Sam's office. He was confused as to why

Sam would accept a random man off the street who appeared to be borderline crazy, so he was curious to find out.

The security guard stared at him briefly before diverting his gaze, and Ross looked down, wondering whether he had any marks or spillages, but, as always, his suit was pristine. He dismissed the matter as he approached Sam's office and stepped through the door.

Part 3 (A)

"So, Sam, what does he need?"

"Did you do this?" Luke held up the newspaper report.

"Yes, that was me."

"I need that."

"No chance."

"What? Why not, you prick? I'll pay you."

"It isn't about money."

"Ross, come here a second," Sam insisted.

Sam led Ross to the other side of the room, leaving Luke out of earshot. Sam was insistent on taking as much business as possible, even if it was risky, as long as he thought it was doable.

"You have to take this," Sam explained.

"Sam, I told you how I feel about these cases."

"You're a lawyer, deal with it."

It wasn't really a decision for Ross; he had to do what Sam said. He reluctantly made his way back to Luke as Sam was welcoming him as a new client. He said they would discuss finances further at a later date and left the two to get acquainted.

Ross leaned against the intricate wooden table while Luke stayed in his chair, staring at Ross. The two studied each other, both sensing a certain familiarity between them but unable to pinpoint it. They sat in silence until Ross pushed off the table and broke the silence.

"If I'm going to help you, I'm going to need to know everything."

"And if I'm going to trust you, I need to know everything."

"There's nothing to know."

"*Everyone has a story.*"

"*Mine really isn't relevant here.*"

"*Are you sure?*"

Just as Luke posed the question, two men in blue police overalls burst into the office, followed by Sam who had tried to stop them but to no avail.

"*Luke Moffat?*" one of them questioned.

"*Yeah.*"

"*You're under arrest.*"

"*For what?*" interjected Ross.

"*Mr Moffat violated rule 4 of his bail and fled to another state.*"

Ross turned to Luke. "*You were on bail?*"

Luke sat in silence.

"*You can't take him. I'm his lawyer.*"

"*You'll have to argue that at the station, sir.*"

"*No.*"

"*Sir, if you could –*"

"*Mr Moffat's representation is in another state; therefore, he is legally allowed to travel states if he wants to talk to his legal counsel in person.*"

"*And who's his lawyer?*"

"*Me.*"

"*Any proof?*"

"*The managing partner of the firm is right behind you. I'm sure he'll be happy to explain.*"

The officers turned towards Sam, who led them out of the office and into a neighbouring conference room so Luke and Ross could finish their introductions but also to distract the officers from the fact that Luke hadn't actually signed as a client yet.

"*What the fuck was that?*"

"*What was what bruv?*"

"*Don't call me bruv. You didn't tell me you were here on bail!*"

"*Yeah, but you sorted it, innit.*"

"*I fucking lied; I have no idea if that's true. It just buys us time.*"

"*Time for what?*"

Ross walked over and took a seat at Sam's table, a table he was destined to inherit someday, so he might as well become accustomed to it now. He made himself comfortable before facing Luke, looking him in the eyes unnervingly.

"*You're going to tell me everything about you.*"

"*No chance.*"

"*If you want me to take your case, you have to tell me everything.*"

"*What do you wanna know?*"

"*Start from the beginning.*"

The two had an in-depth conversation about their backgrounds and where they had come from. Both were careful not to expose everything about themselves, but the similarities between them were clear. Both had broken childhoods and deep trauma, scars that created demons they hadn't been able to fight off. The two found comfort in talking to each other. Until that time, neither had ever had anyone to properly listen to the things they'd been through, and although this was a professional relationship, it was clear it could be so much more. They could understand each other in a way they could not express, but neither revealed their feelings for fear the other did not feel the same energy. Ross had a few last questions for Luke.

"*This question is the most important one I'll ask you.*"

"*Go for it.*"

Ross got up from his seat and leaned across the table towards Luke, making stark eye contact and focusing on even the tiniest pupil movement. He took a moment before asking his question.

"*I'm only going to ask you once. Have you ever killed anyone?*"

"*No.*"

Ross stared at him for a moment, but Luke didn't give anything away. Ross slowly moved back and settled into the chair, adjusting out his suit. He was a perfectionist and always had to cover every detail to make sure he was successful. It worked for him, and he trusted Luke here.

"With that done, we're all good. Welcome to the firm, Luke."

"Cheers."

Laughing, Ross extended an arm to Luke and the pair exchanged a firm handshake. They felt the similar nature in their touch as they had in their eyes.

"Let's get to work."

2 WEEKS LATER

Ross strolled into the prestigious but tainted offices of Walker Malcolm. He had been working his first proper client's case for the past two weeks, and to his surprise, it had gone quite well. There wasn't much evidence incriminating Luke, apart from witness statements, which wasn't enough to go to trial. Luke was always suspicious of the members of the influencer household and kept his tracks well-hidden to avoid situations like this. Ross had been able to not only fight off the case but also claim compensation, claiming that the entire case was slander. Today was the day he was to close the case for good after just submitting his appeal to the court trying to push the counter through.

He waltzed through the office and snaked his way confidently through to conference room B where he would be meeting the state's lawyer, Gemma Harris. She was known for her stubbornness and effectiveness in negotiating deals for them, but they only used her when they were in a losing position, as was the case here.

Blessed with slick black hair and an exceptional but deceiving smile, Gemma was waiting patiently in the conference room as Ross strolled in.

For someone reportedly so dangerous, her look was remarkably innocent. She sat at the conference table, already making herself at home with a cup of piping hot tea. She looked up at Ross as he entered the room, making him feel as though he was being analysed.

"Who are you? Where's Brandon?" he asked.

"They sent me. Please sit."

She gestured to the seat in front of her as if she was the one on home ground and Ross was the away side coming in. Until this point, Ross had been up against Brandon, the deputy district attorney, who had been an easy match for Ross, but this new girl had an intimidating calmness about her. Noticing that Luke hadn't yet arrived, he excused himself from the room to make a phone call. He dialled Luke's number and got no answer. He wasn't too stressed; Luke was normally late. But then Luke rang him.

"Luke, where are you?"

"Ross, I fucked up. I need help!"

"What? What's happened?"

"Nothing, I'm fucking with you." Luke screamed with laughter.

"What the fuck is wrong with you!"

"Just fucking around – I'm round the corner."

Luke appeared, waving at Ross, and calmly walked over to him.

"Do you never take anything seriously?" asked Ross.

"Only serious stuff."

"Let's go in – come on."

Ross led the way back into the conference room and the pair walked in.

"Where's the other guy?" Luke asked.

"Brandon was assigned to another case. I'm Gemma."

She extended a hand to Luke, which he accepted, looking into her eyes. What Ross had found strange and awkward, he found attractive and intriguing. He took a seat, still making eye contact with her. Ross darted a questioning look at the two before also sitting down and drawing the attention of the room to the case.

"Regardless of the change, the case remains the same. There is not enough evidence to tie my client to the things he has been accused of. We will be countersuing, as well, for defamation of character."

Gemma chuckled.

"God, you're such a lawyer. Let me finish my tea." She and Luke chuckled.

Ross glared at Luke, stood up, leaned across the table and slammed his fist down in front of Gemma. She looked petrified. He took a step back, shocked at what he had just done. Still stunned, he retreated further and exited the office. Luke tried to follow him, but Ross urged him back.

Ross went around the corner, his hands shaking and his breathing rapid; he was having a panic attack. Ross rarely had outbursts like that, but they were becoming more frequent and he was afraid. He didn't know how to control his aggression, which was beginning to impact his job. He took a moment to compose himself, taking deep breaths and repeatedly counting to ten, to the confusion of onlookers around the office.

Back in the conference room, Gemma edged closer to Luke, who was looking perplexed.

"I know you did it."

"Don't know what you're talking about."

"I know everything about you, Luke. You're a scumbag, in all honesty. You'll get what's coming to you."

The initial energy between the two had manifested in tension, with Gemma tilting her head to one side and smiling.

"Why are you smiling?"

"What?"

Luke took a second look at her, and Gemma stared at him with the same intensity as before. Luke was wondering what she was up to when her eyes darted to the entrance of the room. Ross walked in calmly.

"Let's continue."

Ross wasted no time in opening up his detailed notes, which he had remembered this time. Luke tried to get a word in to Ross, but he quickly shut him down, eager to continue. He presented three documents with a flourish and laid them on the table, each making a satisfying sound as they landed on the glossy surface. Ross's style was slick and professional; he always attacked and was never on the back foot. His case was strong; there was no new evidence against Luke for this case to continue, but he also offered Gemma the chance to settle. If she paid Luke a small settlement, they would drop their slander suit.

Gemma evaluated the offer in front of her. She took her time in examining the papers until Ross grew impatient.

"Well then?" Ross asked, curbing his emotion this time.

"Yes, we'll settle…"

"Fuck yes!" Luke exclaimed as Gemma smirked.

"She's hiding something," Ross explained with a dry look.

"Right again, Mr Susans. Did you really think I would take that long to read all that?"

Her watch let off a sound, at which she smiled.

"And now, it's done."

"What's done?" asked Luke.

Suddenly, a group of policemen stormed the conference room, followed by Sam yet again trying to stop them. One of the men dragged Luke off his chair and slammed him on the table as Ross and Sam objected.

"*Luke Moffat, you're under arrest on suspicion of the murder of Callum Maratunde.*"

"*What the fuck?*" yelled Luke.

Ross stayed silent, staring into Luke's eyes, as Sam continue to argue. He had lied to him. Ross turned around and walked out of the conference room.

"*Ross!*" Luke screamed. "*Ross, I didn't do shit. This is bullshit. Ross! I did fuck all man. Ross!*"

Ross ignored Luke and walked right out of the building, taking a seat outside to process the rapid-fire events which had caught him massively off guard. He had been out lawyered by Gemma, a rare occurrence. He looked down at his shaking hands and practised his breathing techniques, which relaxed his body. He could not believe that Luke had lied to him. He knew now that he was guilty; it was obvious from his eyes. He slammed the bench with his fist and sat in silence, looking around at a dark, bleak New York. He began to think about where he had come from, all the situations he had experienced, and stumbled upon Reece's death. He took a deep breath as he recalled the moment he'd walked into his room and found him lying there, his face pale and his personality stripped. His train of thought was interrupted by a commotion in front of the building as Luke was evicted, with words flying everywhere and Sam stepping in to fill in Ross's role.

Luke was bundled into the police car and whisked away. Ross walked sheepishly over Sam.

"*You're dropping this case,*" Sam insisted.

"*What?*" Ross said, shocked.

"*We both know he did it, and I'm not having my firm lose a murder case.*"

"*You unloyal bastard.*"

"*Unloyal? I made you in this firm, and you'll do as I say.*"

"*No.*"

"Excuse me?"

Sam took a step closer to Ross.

"No," Ross repeated, defiantly.

"Hang on – why do you want this so bad? You didn't even want this case."

"He's innocent."

"Bullshit, we both know he did it."

"He's innocent."

"Oh, I get it. You two formed a little friendship."

"No that's not it –"

"You can't be friends with a murderer, Ross. Drop the case."

Sam gave him a patronising pat on the shoulder and walked back into the firm, leaving Ross on his own in the New York darkness. He wanted to scream, but nothing came out. Instead, it was an internal scream wreaking havoc inside his head. He stood for a moment, took one final look at the building where he had started his career and walked away.

Part 3 (B)

Luke was dragged into the police station and pushed straight into the interrogation room. The officers handcuffed him to the isolated metal seat in the middle of the room and promptly left him, locking the door behind them. The room was the same as all the others he had seen. He knew their tactics, too, and was undaunted by them as he sat confidently in the chair, knowing he was being watched.

There was no clock in the room, so Luke had no idea how long he had been waiting but it felt like hours. Luke knew they were just trying to get to him and he remained calm. Eventually, the lock clicked and the door swung open to reveal a man dressed in black trousers and a simple white shirt with a notepad and pen in the pocket. Luke inspected him and decided he couldn't be the detective. He stood at roughly 5'7 and didn't look menacing in the slightest. Luke welcomed him as he took a few steps into the room.

"Don't be shy, little buddy," he chuckled.

"Little buddy?" The detective responded with a deep voice that caught Luke by surprise. He pulled out his notepad and started scribbling away, occasionally looking up at Luke. His voice was intimidating, but his appearance was bland and innocent. As Luke tried to figure him out, he abruptly stopped writing, put away the notepad and clasped his hands together in front of Luke.

"Why are you here, Luke?"

"You tell me."

"I know you did this – it's all over your face."

"I haven't done anything. I'm innocent."

"Oh, really, now? Wait until I tell you who tied you to this crime."
"Who?"

Ross sprinted into the police station. He'd realised the ramifications for Luke were huge and he had to save him. He announced himself as he walked in and demanded to see Luke. He tried to barge his way through but was halted by officers as a sergeant stepped in to stop the commotion.

"Excuse me, sir!" the sergeant shouted.

"I demand to see my client, now!"

"He's being interviewed."

"Let me see him now."

"No sir, this is an ongoing murder investigation."

"I'm his goddamn lawyer!"

"He hasn't asked for his lawyer."

"Who are you?" came a voice from behind him.

Ross turned. Two ladies stood behind him. Clearly a mother and daughter, they expressed a fabulous fashion sense but also a sense of strength and unity. Ross worked out from her accent that the two were British.

"Ross Susans. Who are you?"

"Are you Luke Moffat's lawyer?"

"Yes, who are you?"

There was an eruption from the interrogation room behind them as the detective stormed out with Luke in front of him.

"Give me my client."

Ross stepped over to the detective and grabbed Luke out of his grasp.

"What's your name?"

"Detective Alfie Barnes."

"Good to know."

Ross looked him up and down before marching out of the station with Luke. The two ladies stared after them.

As the pair made their way onto the street, Ross led Luke round a corner, out of public sight, and pinned him up against the wall.

"What the fuck is wrong with you? You lied to me!"

"I'm innocent," Luke grunted.

"You're full of shit."

Ross relaxed his grip on Luke as he collapsed to the ground. Ross turned away in disgust as Luke sorted himself out and eventually stood up.

"Listen to me."

"No, Luke, I'm going to win this because I have to. But after this, we're done."

2 Days Later

Luke stood dressed in a stylish suit with even his hair sorted into a parting as he waited in the conference room for Ross to arrive. Today he would be charged with the murder of Callum Maratunde. The case had been brought forward by Alicia and Samantha Maratunde, daughter and wife of the late Callum Maratunde whom Luke had killed just before he fled Mexico, which seemed so long ago now.

Luke was very early and made himself comfortable in the chair as he waited for Ross. The two had had limited contact over the past two days, with Ross willing to discuss only work-related things, but the dynamic of their relationship had drastically changed. Both were unsure of what to expect, and Ross had also found that the opposing counsel had changed at the last minute, so he didn't know whom he was coming up against.

Luke was staring at his phone when he heard footsteps coming into the conference room. They belonged to Samantha and Alicia.

The two paused at the entrance as they stared at Luke, and he wasn't afraid to stare back at them. Luke had always thought he'd done the right thing after what Callum had done to his family, but for years he had thought he had also killed Samantha, his wife. However, she stood strong in front of him but with a noticeable hint of fear in her body. The two stepped into the room and took a seat opposite Luke, without their lawyer.

"*Where's your lawyer?*"

"*We wanted to talk to you first,*" Samantha explained.

"*Not without Ross.*"

"*Shut up, you pig,*" Alicia snapped.

"*What the fuck did you say to me?*"

"*I'll come back for you; do you remember that?*"

"*No.*"

"*Well, now I'm coming for you. You're scum.*"

Alicia spat at Luke and narrowly missed him. She had been just a child when it happened, and it had affected her deeply. Now, as a volatile teenager, she could not miss the chance to fire a shot at Luke.

"*Look, ladies, you've got the wrong guy.*"

"*No. I remember your face. You have distinctive eyes, and I will avenge my husband.*"

"*Your husband? He was a rapist and a murderer!*"

"*Stop! You will not say another bad word about Callum! He was innocent.*"

"*He raped my sister and killed my mum.*"

"*That isn't true!*" Alicia objected.

"*Listen, you little shit –*"

Luke was cut off by Ross who burst into the room and halted Luke mid-sentence, instructing him to sit down as he went around him and took his seat next to him.

"*Where's your lawyer?*" Ross asked.

"*Right here,*" said a foreign voice in the hallway, but not foreign to Ross.

A short-haired blonde appeared from round the corner with the same piercing blue eyes Ross had looked into so many times. It was Chloe Mitchener. She swaggered in with her normal confidence and pulled up a chair next to Alicia, keeping her eyes on Ross, her normal tactic.

"*Good evening, gentlemen. Thank you for the first offer of settlement.*"

"*We feel this is an issue that should be solved quickly with little fuss.*"

"*Oh, I'm sorry. I meant thank you for the offer, but we will not be settling.*"

"*What? This is a settlement meeting, Chloe.*"

"*No, this is a statement, Mr Susans. We went for jail time, maximum penalty, with no parole. Your client is sick and evil.*"

"*Let's be reasonable here. No jailtime.*"

"*Jailtime or no settlement at all.*"

"*Chloe!*"

"*Mr Susans!*"

Luke tapped Ross on the shoulder.

"*Do you know her?*" he whispered.

"*Mr Susans and I were at law school together, Mr Moffat.*"

"*I wasn't asking you.*"

Chloe sat back in her seat, slightly stunned by Luke's snappy response. She sifted through her notes as Luke and Ross had a short whispered argument before composing themselves. The pair were at loggerheads. Every conversation they had ended in an argument, and the tension was visible to all, not the best situation in the middle of a murder case. Chloe simply observed the two bickering like brothers as Ross eventually set up his defence. He used the same gimmick he had used with Gemma, dashing three documents onto the table in front of him, still tainted from the meeting before.

Chloe picked them up and examined them.

"*There is no evidence linking my client to the crime, as you can see.*"

"*I have two witnesses here,*" Chloe said.

"*Yes, your two witnesses. Samantha Maratunde?*"

"*Yes?*"

"*Is it true you were diagnosed with dementia in 2022?*"

"*Yes but –*" Samantha tried.

"*Is it also true that one of the drawbacks of dementia is remembering the wrong version of events?*"

"*Yes but –*"

"*Then it is entirely possible you are misidentifying my client.*"

"*It was him! He has the devil in his eyes, I can see it.*" She stared at Luke who returned a smile.

"*That's your word against his. And Alicia?*"

"*What do you want?*" she fired back.

"*You were a child when this happened. It would have been impossible to identify my client.*"

"*He's not your fucking client, he is a killer. You know it as well.*"

"*My client is innocent.*"

Chloe stayed quiet throughout this encounter, which confused Luke. Lawyers would normally jump in at these points, but she simply observed, which made him think she had another move up her sleeve.

"*You are correct; both of my witnesses' testimonies can be faulted.*"

"*So, you concede defeat? Already! Wow, you really went downhill after Harvard. The Chloe I know would never let this go.*"

"*I'm not the same Chloe, Ross. But you are still Mr Susans, and once again you've let your arrogance get the better of you.*"

Chloe had a smug smile on her face, and Samantha with Alicia
looked more cocky than usual. Luke and Ross both realised they
had something else. After satisfying her urge to see them in panic
mode, Chloe revealed her trump card.

A young man walked into the office wearing an oversized suit.
Neither Luke nor Ross recognised him as he nervously walked in
at Chloe's summons and took a seat on her left.

"Who's this?"

"This is Andrew Teare. From Stratford."

"How is he relevant here?"

"I'll let him explain."

"I prefer to go by Drew," he said meekly.

"Shut up you rat. Tell the story," snarled Luke.

"I saw you."

"Me?"

Luke examined his face, scouring through his records of his
enemies. He couldn't locate the man, which made him think this
was a bluff from Raquel. He shot up from his chair and accused
Chloe of witness tampering and lying. Chloe looked up at him in
disbelief.

"He saw you at the stairs of Callum's estate," she whispered.

Suddenly, Luke recognised the man. His face had changed a
lot, but he had the same eyebrows and nervous exterior. He was
one of the boys who had been scared away when Luke stormed the
estate. Luke glared at him. One rule of play in Luke's world was that
snitches get stitches; he would get revenge on him at some point.

"You'll lose this at trial."

"You don't know that."

"We both know you will, Mr Susans. My settlement is life in
prison."

"Fuck off."

Chloe stood up elegantly and walked out with her three witnesses. Ross and Luke were left in silence.

Luke was worried about going to prison but more about the flashback he'd had a second before. In his history rewind, he had been reminded of all the lives he had taken, not only Callum's. Meanwhile, Ross was stressed about his career. He had now been beaten twice, completely outsmarted by both Gemma and Chloe. He was losing his edge. And there were his recent panic attacks and outbursts of anger. Then a thought occurred to him.

"*How did they get Chloe?*"

"*What bruv?*"

"*How did they get her? She's a corporate lawyer. They live on an estate.*"

"*Ah fuck.*"

"*Who is it?*"

"*Sean Davis.*"

"*Who's that?*"

"*My old boss. He wants me dead. He must be coming for me through this.*"

"*Fuck sake, Luke!*"

"*How is this my fault?*"

"*You're a fucking murderer!*"

"*I killed him because he raped my sister and killed my mother!*"

The two were now standing inches apart, with the tension so heightened even the room was paying attention. It was looking as if an actual fight was about to occur when Sam waltzed into the room and stood between them.

"*What's wrong with you two? Acting like children.*"

"*We're fucked, Sam.*"

"*You didn't drop the case?*"

"*Drop the fucking case?*" shouted Luke.

"You didn't tell him?" Sam asked Ross, to which he made no reply.

"Tell me what? Tell me fucking what!"

"Sam asked me to drop your case," Ross muttered.

"You fucking bastard."

"Luke, listen."

"No, Ross. You sit on this stupid fucking pedestal looking down on everyone like the king of a moral compass – take a look at yourself from time to time, you prick."

Luke stormed off, and Ross didn't bother to go after him. He stared at the ground, acknowledging to himself his guilt and hypocrisy. Sam walked over to him, his anger evident through his exaggerated movements.

"If you don't win this case now, I'll fire you," Sam said unapologetically and rushed out after Luke. Ross sat back down with his head in his hands, wrestling with his emotions. He was all alone again. He had lost himself, and it had finally caught up with him. He knew exactly who he needed to speak to.

Outside, Luke was a man on a mission. Sam was hot on his tail, trying to slow him down, knowing he had intentions of doing something rash.

"Luke, stop!" yelled Sam.

"Piss off."

"What will you do? Kill that boy? That isn't going to solve anything."

"It's about respect."

"No, it's not. There's more to life than your petty arguments with children. Grow up!"

"You have no idea what I've been through."

"Been through? You grew up in Chelsea, for God's sake."

"I meant the life I live!"

"A life that you chose!"

That silenced Luke. The life he was living was of his own making. He'd never been forced into it. He chased it; he was enthralled by it. The consequences of his actions had finally caught up with him, and he wasn't going to get out of it this time.

"If you know what's good for you, you'll turn yourself in!"

"I didn't do this."

"Enough with the bullshit!"

"I'm innocent. I will fight."

"Don't drag Ross down with you."

"I'm innocent."

"Get out of my sight."

Luke scuttled away from Sam, disappearing into the darkness. He slipped away into the unknown, leaving Sam and Ross behind. He had one goal.

Ross exited the lift and turned to exit the building but was caught by Sam on his return. He looked Ross dead in the eye.

"You're going to cost me my firm."

"A leader doesn't blame his workers for his shortcomings."

"I made you in this firm."

"Oh, so that's how it is?"

"You're goddamn right that's how it is!"

"You made me take this case!"

"And I am taking it away now!"

"No."

"What's wrong with you? He's a murderer."

"But this was ok when he was just a dealer? Is that where we draw the moral line?"

"Either you drop this, or you're fired."

"Fuck you."

Sam barged past Ross and made his way to the lifts. He turned to Ross as the ding echoed through the deserted hallway.

"You've got a week."

Ross cursed under his breath and walked onto the street, looking around to see if there was anyone near him. He had no idea who Luke's enemies were, and they could be hunting him as a target. He took out his phone and skimmed through his contact list, but there was no one he could really call. Everyone on the list was either out of his life or dead. He scrolled down past Isaac and Tyler, both now distant memories in his life. In all the commotion he had lost who he truly was, that boy from Harold Wood with a dream to buy his mum a house and now he hadn't spoken to her in over a year. He went to sit on a bench to compose himself. His face was grey and his once glossy hair had lost its sheen. His eyes, once filled with wonder and a sense of opportunity, were now filled with guilt and regret.

When did he change into this man that he disliked so much? He tried his phone again and scrolled further down the contact list, reaching a name and reluctantly hitting call. The phone rang for a few seconds before the person picked up.

"*Hello Ross?*" the female voice said.

"*I need to speak to you.*"

Simultaneously, Luke was on the hunt for Andrew Teare. People had always questioned Luke's approach, labelling him as violent and overly aggressive, but it was to prevent situations like this from popping up. He had gathered the address of the hotel where Andrew was staying, but he knew he had to be careful as he would be heavily guarded by witness protection, especially given Luke's reputation. He chose to travel on foot instead of by taxi, moving in stealth and silence.

He approached the Park Lane Hotel, a lavish establishment located not far from Times Square and popular among British tourists. He didn't have a clear plan, but when did he ever. He decided to hide in plain sight and entered through the front entrance, which was watched by two beefy security guards. He took little notice of them, but they caught his exhaustion as he stepped into the brightly lit lobby.

As always, Luke was out of place in the grand hotel. The lobby was decorated in a classy white with a glossy finish, and in the middle stood a black sculpture with a fountain. He made his way to reception, which was deserted. Almost too easy.

"Hey, sorry I've lost my room key," Luke explained.

"Of course, sir. What's the room number?"

"Sorry, it's slipped my mind. The name is Andrew Teare."

"One moment, sir."

The attendant picked up the phone and began to dial. Luke did a quick survey of the room and noticed four pairs of eyes trained on him from various corners of the lobby. He was being watched. As the attendant put down the phone, Luke noticed that the man closest to him had started to move towards him. It was the man from the newspaper stand in the subway in Los Angeles. The man reached out to him and Luke closed his eyes in fear of the unknown. His eyes remained shut as the attendant called him again. Luke slowly opened his eyes and looked around him, pivoting on the spot to the attendant's confusion. He did another scan of the room and found no one was remotely interested in what he was doing. The men he had seen before had vanished.

"Sir!" the attendant demanded for the fifth time.

"Yes, sorry. Daydreaming innit."

"Right... I'll need to see some identification."

Luke patted himself, looking for an ID that he knew he didn't have.

"Sorry, I must have left it in the room."

"I can't give you a key without identification, sir."

"Fuck sake!"

"Excuse me, sir?"

Luke steadied himself. This time, his shout had drawn the attention of those in the lobby and, more importantly, the security guards at the front door. They had taken a step inside, with their eyes in the direction of reception.

"It's ok, I'll try and sort some ID."

"Sir."

"It's ok."

"Security!"

"You fucking bitch."

Luke shot off down the lobby, aiming for the side door. He knew being caught would heavily impact his case. Luke was of impressive size but lacked the build of the security guards, so his only option was to try and escape.

He was closely pursued by the men, who had split up, causing Luke to lose track of them. He passed through the hotel at a walking pace so as not to draw too much attention to himself, and security did the same so as not to cause panic among the guests. Luke quickly formulated a plan to lose the two in the hotel's restaurant. He simply walked past the attendant at the front, who tried to call him back, and sprinted towards the kitchen. As he picked up the pace the men did too. Luke used his speed and agility to navigate his way delicately through the tables.

He leapfrogged over the buffet counter at full pelt, drawing gasps from around the restaurant, before brushing past two chefs and storming into the kitchen. The other chefs stared at him quizzically before returning to work.

Luke did a quick scan of the kitchen and found what he was looking for, a fire exit. As he dashed towards it, the two security guards bursting through the kitchen doors. Luke dropped to the ground at the feet of one of the chefs. The Chinese man looked down at Luke, who lifted his finger to his lips.

"Has anyone come through here?" demanded a guard.

"No," stated the chef.

"Are you sure?"

"Positive."

The guards made a half-hearted attempt to find Luke and gave up. Luke had escaped. He looked up and smiled at the chef who had spared him without even knowing him or what his situation was. The chef, brimming with compassion, smiled back. Luke reached into his pocket, pulled out $20 and handed it to the chef. The chef smiled in amazement and offered Luke an arm up, which he gratefully accepted. Luke cracked a smile, possibly his first ever genuine one. The chef pulled him in for a hug to Luke's surprise, but he didn't push him away; he appreciated the warmth.

"Now go!" the chef insisted, pushing him away and handing back the money.

"Please take it."

"If you do nice things in a hope of a return, then it isn't a nice thing."

"Thank you."

With that, Luke made his way to the fire exit, with the other chefs taking little notice of events. He took one last look at the man behind him, gave him another smile, which the chef reciprocated, and disappeared into the night.

His eyes took a moment to adjust to the darkness as he walked down the fire escape and into a side alley adjacent to the hotel. Raising the hood of his hoodie, he stepped into the street, which was bright and bustling with life. He took a look around and saw a commotion at the entrance to the hotel. It was the guards still searching for him, so he ducked back into the alley and crouched behind a bin. As the commotion died down, he heard the footsteps of two individuals coming down the alley towards him.

He peeked out over the bin to see who they were, but he couldn't make them out in the dark. They walked halfway down the alley and stopped, within earshot, at the foot of the fire escape where he had exited moments before.

"*What's the issue?*" one of the shadows asked.

"*I'm scared.*"

Luke recognised the voice. It was Andrew.

"*Scared of what?*"

Luke couldn't make out the other shadow's voice, but he recognised it.

"*You know, him. He's a madman.*"

"*Listen, he isn't shit. Just a ponced-up fanny in a hoodie trying to be something he isn't.*"

"*What the fuck did you say?*" shouted Luke shouted, leaping up from his spot.

"*Luke?*" The shadow stepped forward to reveal Detective Alfie Barnes.

"*Damn right it's Luke.*"

"*What the fuck are you doing here?*"

Luke came a few steps closer to the detective until their noses were practically touching. Andrew stood backed against the wall.

"*I've dealt with your kind before – you're nothing,*" the detective jeered.

"*You've never seen anything like me before.*"

"*A failed man who abandoned his family to chase a silly high, with no friends and no relationship at the age of 25. I've seen a million of you.*"

"*That's not me,*" Luke whispered.

"*You let your sister get raped and your mum get killed. You're an embarrassment to your family and humanity. Your dad would be ashamed.*"

Luke took a swing at the detective, but he had anticipated it and took a step back. He struck Luke in the stomach and kicked him to the ground. Luke forced himself up and pushed the detective to the ground. He managed to get on top of him and landed several heavy blows to his face until blood glistened on his hand.

Luke showed no sign of slowing down. Andrew remained with his back to the wall, too scared to run in case he ended up the same way. The detective just managed to open his eyes, which were swollen and smeared with blood. He looked Luke in the eye.

"*This life you so desperately crave, it only ends one way. You'll lose.*"

"*I never lose.*"

"*That's not what I meant.*"

Luke gave one final punch to the detective's skull and his eyes closed. Andrew let out a muffled scream, too scared to even cry. Luke straightened up and approached his real target.

He grabbed Andrew by the neck and slammed him against the wall. The thump echoed around the alleyway.

"*You little prick,*" Luke said, the detective's blood still dripping down his arms.

"*Luke... please.*" Andrew struggled to get his words out as he gasped for air.

"*You're a fucking snake, and now you'll go where snakes belong. Under the fucking grass!*"

Luke tightened his grip on Andrew's neck as he continued to struggle, his legs now jerking vigorously in an attempt to escape. His eyes began to roll to the back of his head. Just as Luke was about to complete his mission, a bright beam of light shone from the top of the alleyway. Luke relaxed his grip, allowing Andrew to collapse to the floor and gasp for air. After Luke's eyes had adjusted to the glare, he managed to make out three silhouettes. The police. Luke cursed under his breath. He had no choice but to flee, despite the fact that Andrew was still breathing.

"*I'll be back for you.*"

With that, Luke raised his hood over his head and sprinted down the opposite side of the alleyway, disappearing into the darkness yet again.

Elsewhere, Ross had a mission of his own. He had to get to Boston. He was on his way to meet the mystery lady whom he had phoned. He hopped on a plane at New York International Airport and embarked on the short but tedious one-hour flight to Boston. The flight gave him some time to relax and reflect on the chaos of his life before the wheels scraped the runway. He had touched down in Boston.

He swiftly made his way through airport security, carrying just his rucksack; he did not plan on staying long. He exited the airport and located the nearest taxi, instructing the driver to take him to Harvard University. The drive was brief and, for the most part, uneventful. Ross sat silently in the back, looking out of the window and admiring the area where he had lived for the better part of three years, a place filled with memories from the good to the bad to the awful. Memories of the exciting times he had experienced came rushing back, from the amazing times he had spent with Tyler to the mock trial rivalry with Chloe. Ross missed it, but the city didn't have the same glow as before. To him, it appeared drained and bleak, almost as if someone had cast a curse over it.

Along with all the exciting and happy memories sat some deep-rooted painful ones that had very much shaped Ross into the person he was today. The taxi glided past his old apartment and the hill where he had spent so much time. His mind flashed back to Jazmine, all the time he had spent with her and how much he had done for her, and she had done for him. He missed her, her smile, her innocence, her pure beauty, not to mention her ability to make sure everything would be ok no matter the situation. She had been the first person to accept Ross as he was. Not only had she broken his heart, she had broken him.

The taxi pulled up outside the grand entrance of Harvard University. As an alumnus, Ross was always welcomed back, despite his distaste for the place. He had been very successful here, having finished top of his class in every subject apart from one – Ethics. Ross made his way through the entrance. The school day had ended and the place was unusually empty. His footsteps echoed as he made his way through the halls he had travelled down so many times as a student, rushing to lectures or to hand in assignments. Life had been so much simpler then, yet it seemed so stressful at the time. He was a different person entirely, but he couldn't figure out where it had changed for him.

At the end of a hallway, he arrived at the room he had been targeting. He composed himself, took a deep breath and knocked gently.

"Come in!" the female voice called.

Ross stepped into the room. The lady was seated at the far end of the classroom, staring at her computer. She wore glasses, and her bright blonde hair was tied into a bun. It was Dr Mansell. Ross made his way down and took a seat opposite her, her eyes still fixed on the screen in front of her. The two had had a good relationship during Ross's time at Harvard, but their friendship had deteriorated due to conflicting opinions on certain ethical issues. He had held a grudge against her for years, feeling she'd let their personal relationship affect the professional one, but he was stuck. He didn't know who else to turn to for advice in the situation in which he now found himself. Ross sat patiently waiting for her to finish. It was almost as though she stayed silent on purpose. After a few minutes, she calmly closed her laptop screen, clasped her hands together and turned her attention to him.

"What is this about Ross?"

"I need your advice."

"You didn't want it two years ago."

"Please."

"Go on."

Ross told her the whole story about Luke, including the fact that he now knew that he was a murderer but if he didn't take the case, he would lose his job. Dr Mansell took off her glasses and leaned back in her chair as Ross gave her all the details. She gave a loud sigh and took a moment to think about what she had just been told before she spoke.

"Do you remember your last day here, graduation day?"

"How is that relevant?"

"Do you remember it?"

"Of course I do."

"When I watched you go up to get your degree, there was not a hint of happiness in your face."

"I was tired."

"No. You chose money. You sold yourself to the devil to be in a flashed-up suit in a corporate office protecting your rich clients and not caring about who you screwed up in the process."

"That's not true."

"You lost yourself. When you first walked into my classroom, all you wanted to do was help people. I don't even recognise you anymore."

"Neither do I," Ross muttered.

"The only advice I can give you is you've got a choice. Either you find inner peace and leave this tainted job. Or, you keep your money and your easy lifestyle but live with the demon the rest of your life. But hey, at least you'll have money!"

Ross slammed his fist on the desk in frustration and stormed off. That was exactly what he didn't want to hear. But deep down, he knew she was right. He was trying to run and couldn't face the fact that he was wrong.

"*You can't run forever!*" she called out after him.

Ross slammed the door, stamped through the empty hallway, and gave a roar of frustration. The commotion he was causing was bound to attract attention. A door opened in front of him and a woman stepped out. She had sun-streaked brown hair partnered with piercing blue eyes and a gleaming smile. It was Jaz.

Ross froze. He looked at her for the first time in years and all the memories came flooding back, as well as the emotions which had been buried deep in his heart. He hadn't dealt with his pain, he had simply pushed it to one side, and he couldn't deal with it now. Her beauty dazzled him, and he was just stunned to be in her presence again, even after what she had done to him.

"*Ross? What are you doing here?*"

"*Hey,*" he whispered, his anger instantly dispersing.

"*Hi,*" she gently responded.

"*What are you doing here?*" she repeated.

"*I came to see Dr Mansell. What about you?*"

"*I work here now. I'm a lecturer.*"

"*Oh wow. Well done.*"

"*How have you been?*"

"*Better now I'm talking to you,*" he said with a smile.

She paused.

"*What?*" Ross asked, sensing something was off.

As the word left his mouth, a man appeared behind Jazmine, putting his arms around her waist. It was the same man he had seen that night at the club.

"*Who's this, honey?*" the man asked.

A dagger ripped through Ross's heart again. Just when he thought he might have something back in his life that could bring him some sort of joy, it was ripped away from him in an instant. He simply nodded a few times, keeping eye contact with Jaz, before turning to walk away, not looking back, as much as he was tempted to. He felt the tears forming in his eyes but pushed them right to the back of his head. He had a job to do.

Part 3 (C)

Three months had passed since Ross had seen Jaz with her new boyfriend and Luke had killed detective Barnes. Today was the most important day in both their lives. It was trial day. Ross had decided to go through with the case despite his moral objections that had tried to force him away. Luke hadn't been charged or even associated with the murder of Detective Alfie Barnes, but he also hadn't told Ross he had killed him. Luke was playing a dangerous game but was not prepared to tell Ross for fear that he would drop his case.

The two had planned to meet at Ross's apartment before the trial. Ross had suggested it so they could both get in the right headspace before going to such a big event. There was immense pressure, particularly on Ross, who had to deal with a heartbreak as well as all the pressures of the case and Luke, who wasn't exactly the ideal client. He pushed all this to the back of his mind, as he always did. He was focused on winning and moving forward. It was also a chance for a last conversation, in a sense, just in case things didn't pan out the way they had planned.

Luke arrived at Ross's building unusually dressed in a suit. He had put noticeable effort into his appearance as if the seriousness of his actions had finally caught up with him and he was ready to face the consequences. He took the elevator to the 50th floor where Ross resided. He stepped out of the elevator, receiving looks from people in the corridor because of his exaggerated appearance, or maybe it was the guilt so clearly written on his face. He ignored the onlookers, as he always did, and knocked on the door of apartment 57. There was no response to his first knock, so he knocked again. The door creaked open as Luke gave it a push. Ross was not standing by the door ready to let him in but sitting on his abnormally expensive black sofa overlooking the New York skyline, with a glass of whiskey placed delicately on the table in front of him. It was half-empty. He was half-dressed as well.

As Luke entered the room, Ross paid no attention to him, his focus on the view rather than the pressing issue at hand. It was as though he was afraid to even face Luke. Luke didn't show the same nervousness, he never had, as he charged across the room and took a seat opposite him. Ross still refused to look at him. Luke stared at the man who was meant to be representing him in a few hours and didn't seem to care. Luke was stunned. It was his trial day, one of the most important days in his life, and his lawyer appeared uninterested.

"*Ross!*" he shouted, to no response.

After repeated attempts to rouse Ross, he lost his temper and slammed his fist on the table, causing Ross's glass to topple. That finally grabbed his attention.

"*Sorry… I was daydreaming.*"

"*Daydreaming? On my trial day? Get yourself in gear!*"

"*Sorry. I just…*"

"*It's 10 am and you're sat here with a half-empty glass of whiskey!*"

"*It's half-full.*"

"*What difference does that fucking make!*"

"*Perspective is everything,*"

"*Are you drunk?*"

Ross looked out to the skyline again.

"*You're fucking drunk! On the most important day of my life!*"

"*You don't understand.*"

"*Understand what? That you're an incompetent lawyer?*"

"*You don't understand.*"

"Fucking explain it then!" Luke rose from his seat with his arms outstretched and violence etched all over his face.

"I can't."

"Tell me, you prick!"

Ross looked him in the eye, hiding the tears so as not to appear weak.

"Sit down."

"Why?"

"Sit down and I'll tell you."

Luke calmed down and slowly descended onto the sofa. Ross's eyes had lost their spark; the light had faded in them. As Ross looked back at Luke, he saw that his eyes didn't have the spark that Ross's once had but they had changed. They were filled with atonement and forgiveness, something Ross had never noticed before.

"Go on then," Luke said more calmly.

"I have some advice for you."

"What's that?"

Ross leaned forward in his chair.

"Whatever you do, never fall in love."

"I never intend to," Luke snapped back.

"Why?"

"How can I love someone when I hate myself?"

Ross leaned back in his chair and contemplated what Luke had just told him. He realised that maybe the two were more alike than he'd thought. He had always viewed Luke as the raging madman society had labelled him, who didn't care about anyone but himself, but maybe he was just a misunderstood man in serious pain. Luke started again.

"Pain changes a man. Love is usually the catalyst for that pain. When I was younger, before my dad passed, he always used to tell

me: Be careful of women; they come looking beautiful but can inflict the pain of an army of 1000 men."

"Your dad passed away?" Ross asked.

"Yeah, when I was very young."

"Same."

The two fell into complete silence as they related to each other in a way they never had before. Growing up without a father figure is always difficult, yet here they were, two different individuals, having gone through the same trauma.

"How did he die?" Ross asked.

"Never asked," Luke replied, bluntly.

"Same."

Ross looked down at the floor, tears hitting his silky velvet carpet with the weight of his pain. Luke observed him coldly, with not a sign of a tear. His expression mirrored that of a brick wall, not letting anything in.

Opposites tend to attract, or maybe they were meant to meet each other, despite their differences. Silence filled the room as the two broken men faced each other. Ross eventually gathered the courage to look up at Luke.

"It is ok to cry, you know."

"Society tells me differently."

Ross reached into his suit jacket and drew out an oddly shaped item. A gun. Luke's pupils widened. He had been in similar situations before, but it was the last thing he expected from Ross.

"What the fuck are you doing?"

Ross stayed silent and innocently placed the gun on the table in front of him, twisting it gun intentionally so it pointed toward Luke. Luke couldn't believe that even Ross was going to betray him. He looked into his eyes again, and all he saw was pain, a broken man with a reckless weapon.

"What are you doing Ross?"

"They never tell you how hard it can be. How life isn't fair and the pain you can experience can run so deep it can completely change you as a person."

"Why have you got a gun?"

"You know, I wish I had met you earlier. You're the first client that actually gave a shit about me and that I genuinely thought was a good person."

"I'm not a good person, Ross."

"Neither am I! No one fucking is!"

"Put the gun away. You aren't thinking rationally."

"I just want the pain to end."

"How is killing me going to fix that?"

"The gun was never for you."

"What?"

In a flash, Ross reached for the gun and turned it on himself, fixing the barrel firmly against his head. Luke looked at him, stunned into a statue.

"Ross... please, put the gun down."

"Give me a reason to."

"Ross. Please."

Luke slowly got up with his hands in front of him in a show of surrender.

"There's too much pain."

"It gets better."

"Do you actually believe that?"

Luke was forced into silence because the truth was, he didn't.

"I'm sorry man, I can't."

"You're only adding to the pain in this world if you do this."

"I am the pain in this world."

"Ross. Please. I'm begging you."

"I'm sorry bro."

"Ross. No!"

Ross sweaty finger pulled the trigger faster than Luke could react. The bullet sent a ripple around the apartment almost like Ross's scream. Luke let out a sound but was drowned out by the echo of the bullet. A piece of Luke's heart had been ripped out right in front of him, and the living scream was quickly followed by dead silence. Luke rushed over to him, knowing deep down it was too late; the bullet had ripped through Ross's head, taking his soul with it. Luke clasped his dying body in his arms as the blood flowed down his arms, scarlet, pure and genuine. Luke didn't care about any of that. He simply sat with Ross's body in his arms, looking at a young man who had started with the purest of intentions and had been convinced by others he was evil. The world didn't deserve him.

Luke tried to feel something, but he couldn't. He leant over and whispered something into his ear before closing his eyes. A single tear fell, landing on Ross's eye.

Part 3 (D)

29ᵗʰ December 2028

A light fog descended over the Merton and Sutton cemetery. It was the day of the funeral of Ross Susans, a loving, hardworking man who always liked to see the best in people and never gave up on them, no matter what. He had passed away a month before, and his mother had wished to bury him near his brother so she could come and visit them both. His body was transported back to London with the cost of everything covered by Sam, more out of guilt than the goodness of his heart. Luke managed to get his trial date pushed back, not that he was concerned about that at the moment. It was to be a small ceremony, with Luke and Ross's mum expected to be the only ones in attendance.

Luke hopped out of a taxi and stood facing the gates of the cemetery. He was humbled in the presence of such a grand entrance to such a hollow place. Graveyards are interesting places. Millions of people buried underground along with their ideas, thoughts and feelings. Forever. He had arrived exhausted, straight from the airport. Nevertheless, he had an obligation to be here, to pay his respects in a meaningful way to the only man who had given him a chance.

He trudged through the muddy graveyard filled with the bodies of people with different stories and different-sized holes, both in the ground and in people's lives. This was the only place where people were truly equal, regardless of judgement. He examined a few graves along the way, many of which had flowers and messages on them from family members, friends and even strangers. Luke wondered how many of them had visited out of guilt rather than actual sorrow. He had always believed that no one truly cares until you're dead, and from what he had seen, he was right.

One grave drew his attention. He took a few steps towards it then stopped dead in his tracks as the memory returned to him. It was his dad's grave. He crouched down beside the grave as his mind flashed back to the funeral. He wiped the dirt off the gravestone, revealing what he had suspected. The gravestone read *Harry Moffat, loving father and respected doctor.* He took a moment to sit by his grave, an opportunity he had never taken before. He felt like a child again. He had never visited his grave, mostly because he was scared to see it, not that he would ever admit that to anyone.

He sat twiddling his thumbs, unsure of what to do or what to say. He took another look at the gravestone and noticed a further inscription masked by dust and dirt. He wiped it away to reveal a quote.

'*Don't be sad I am gone; I know my sons will make me proud.*'

He scoffed. He hadn't even got close to the type of man his dad was. He sat and wondered what life might have been like if he was still alive. Would he be proud of him? Luke's heart sank at the realisation that his dad would probably be disgusted at the person he had become. He was shocked to the core. Maybe he was the bad guy all along. He took another look at the quote and was drawn to the word "sons". It confused him, but he assumed it was an error.

This was the first time he had experienced complete silence; not even nature dared make a sound in this place. He looked around the grave and noticed that it had been well maintained, he assumed by Georgia. Another wave of guilt consumed him. He was completely at fault for a massive trauma in her life, but even so, she always looked out for him. He smiled to himself as he stood up.

"I'm sorry, Dad."

With that, he walked off toward Ross's grave, still thinking about all the mistakes he had made and how they had affected the people who really cared about him. He realised he had only acted with selfish intentions and never thought about the trail he left behind, which included several people who lost their lives as a direct result of his actions.

On the other side of the cemetery, a woman dressed in black was standing by the hole that had been dug out for Ross. As Luke slowly approached her, she turned towards him and Luke recognised her. She was Ross's mum; they had the same eyes.

"*Hello Luke,*" she said softly.

"*You know me?*"

"*Ross mentioned you a lot.*"

"*He did?*"

"*We hadn't talked for a while, but he called me a few months ago. He said he had found the most amazing man.*"

"*He didn't mean me.*"

"*You're the only other one here.*"

Luke looked down at the floor.

"*I could have saved him,*" he whispered.

"*You did.*"

"*I didn't.*"

"*Ross thought he was the bad guy. He thought he caused pain and sadness in other people when the truth is, he was just a nice guy in a cutthroat world. You were the first person that came along who didn't abandon him. And you still haven't.*"

She gave Luke a hug and whispered, "*Thank you for showing my son he means something.*"

The hug lasted for a good few minutes as Luke thought about what she had told him. His mind flashed back to his dad's grave stone. He couldn't shake the word "sons" out of his head. Ross's mum pulled away and looked into Luke's soul. It was pure deep down; she was a good judge of character and a strong woman who had been through so much. No parent should ever have to bury their child, definitely not twice.

"*You have his eyes,*" she whispered.

"*No, his were brighter.*"

"*Yours are just as bright; you just don't see it yet.*"

"*He was too good for this world,*" Luke said, staring at the hole.

"*This world never deserved an angel like him.*"

The pair looked at the hole in the ground. It seemed too simple for a body. More than just a body, a whole life.

"*Can you promise me something?*" she asked.

"*Anything.*"

"*Carry on his legacy for me.*"

Luke paused.

"*I'm not the right person for that.*"

"*Not right now, maybe. But I see him in you.*"

Luke looked back at the gaping hole in front of him; it was somehow bigger. All the memories of him came flooding back. His smile, his intelligence, but most importantly, his empathy. No one had ever given Luke a chance. He was written off as a screw-up, but Ross always saw the good in him, even when he was advised against it. He had saved Luke's life, at his own expense.

The fog thickened and a dark emptiness encompassed the graveyard.

"*I'm going to go now,*" Ross's mum said.

"*Alright, be safe.*"

"*I'll see you later.*"

"*You're a good mum.*" He smiled at her.

She returned the smile before walking off as she'd arrived, alone. That left Luke and the hole in the ground.

"*Don't really know what to say here. I've never talked to a grave. I guess I'll start with, I'm sorry. For everything.*"

He stopped himself as he noticed an envelope fluttering in the dirt that was to be used to fill in the grave. He carefully picked it up and looked inside.

Hey, it's Ross.

I guess this is my suicide note, but think of it more like a speech. I preferred to talk. Those who know me well will know what I've been through and the struggle I've been fighting for the past few years. If you're reading this, it means I decided to take my own life. I don't like the word suicide – it's ugly and harsh. First things first, I was not saveable. I've been on a downwards slope since I lost my dad and my brother, Reece. I haven't really known anything else apart from pain, but I couldn't let my mother see it. If you're reading this, mum, you did your best. Please don't shed any tears for me, I really wasn't that special. I love every single one of you that I have had the privilege to meet in my life, even the pricks. The love is still there, it will always be – it's unconditional. That goes for everyone, even those I hurt. I'm sorry. You're all amazing individuals in your own right and have helped me so much in all your unique, brilliant ways. Some of you might be confused, angry or sad; whatever the emotion, don't think about it too much. All I was going to carry around the world was sadness and hatred, and the world has enough of that. I didn't want to burden the rest of you with my problems. I can't live in a world where the people I love always leave or don't get to see the things I am achieving. I don't do it for myself, I do it for others. A part of me has always been missing. None of you should blame yourselves. This is the most important thing. I was never going to win this battle. I know that there are people who love and care about me I just never saw any value in myself as a person. I love each and every one of you.

P.S. Luke, if you're reading this, don't worry. I'll never leave you.

Love,
Ross

Luke collapsed to his knees with the letter gripped in his hands. Tears now flooded out of his eyes as they never had before. The letter was hard to read, and he had so many questions. The only issue was that they were for the man six feet under.

He tucked the letter back into the mud where he had found it. He kneeled down closer to his grave. The rain started to pour down, splattering against Luke and helping hide his tears, even though no one was around. He stared blankly at the scene around him. Desolate and empty. He was the only man for miles, yet he was surrounded by thousands, each with their own story.

He leaned in closer to Ross, not caring about Sean, Raquel or even his case. He removed all the wandering thoughts from his mind and focused on the grave in front of him. He got as close as he could without falling in and gently whispered farewell.

"Rest in paradise, my brother."

"It takes two men to make one brother."

Lightning Source UK Ltd.
Milton Keynes UK
UKHW011849240521
384288UK00001B/4